M.L. Anderson was born in the Rhondda Valley, South Wales. She grew up in Salisbury, Southern Rhodesia where her father worked as an engineer. It was the start of her lifelong passion for travelling. The family returned to England in her late teens settling in Derbyshire where over the years she explored the stunning landscape of the Derbyshire Dales, eventually retiring to live in the area in later life.

Married with children and five grown grandchildren, she and her husband live in the beautiful Peak District where she spends her time writing, gardening and travelling around the world to visit members of the family.

For Len and Joyce and my husband, Ron.

M.L. Anderson

THE SMALL HILL

To Elizabeth
love & Best Wishes
Meryl.

AUSTIN MACAULEY PUBLISHERS™

LONDON • CAMBRIDGE • NEW YORK • SHARJAH

M.L. Anderson.

A CIP catalogue record for this title is available from the British Library.

ISBN 9781398483538 (Paperback)
ISBN 9781398483545 (ePub e-book)

www.austinmacauley.com

First Published 2023
Austin Macauley Publishers Ltd®
1 Canada Square
Canary Wharf
London
E14 5AA

I would like to thank Sir Richard FitzHerbert who made us welcome in his village where I found the inspiration for my story.

Also thank you to our friends, Carole and Kenneth, who made us feel so much at home.

Last and not least I want to thank my son, Max, for his professional help and advice. My daughter, Sue, for her encouragement. Lainie, Ian, Barbara and all the family for cheering me on and a special thank you to my husband, Ron, for all his patience.

Table of Contents

There is a quiet place. A small hill where shadows dwell as clouds float by and silvery grass sways to and fro; where water murmurs along the foot before disappearing out of sight under tangled growth and long-forgotten echoes call.

Centuries ago when men arrived to farm the rich, dark soil and hunt in the surrounding woods they settled near the hill and felt its stillness. They buried their dead on the hillside long before the stone cross was built where Holy men came to preach and the ancient word 'Woeh' was whispered meaning 'Sacred Place'.

I

The Knight stood on the hill looking over the land and wrapped the coarse wool cloak tightly around his aging bones to keep out the chill. His body was wracked with pain and often the ague came upon him. He knew his time was near and soon he would rest near the boy, his beloved son who was buried on the hillside facing the setting sun. He remembered gently touching the boy's cold cheek before going out into the coolness of the evening, to stand on top of the hill watching the sun sink below the horizon and he continued to stand there until dawn.

The Knight felt cold and pulling his cloak tighter, he thought of his first day up on the hill as a young warrior looking out over the land and he knew the hill and the land surrounding it would eventually be his. He had come upon the area by accident, straight from the heat of battle, subduing those rebelling against the authority of his Lord. After he had imposed his will showing no mercy, he remembered riding across the land leading his soldiers towards the distant wooded area. There they found soft grassland below a small hill where fresh water ran; he signalled to his men and they dismounted wearily, dropping down on the ground with fatigue.

After ordering his men to refresh the horses and rest, he began to climb the hill drawn to do so. His shoulder throbbed where he sustained a wound and as he reached the top, he saw a carved stone cross and went over to it. Sinking to the ground, he rested against the cold, rough granite surface, his head full of thoughts and images he could not manage.

He eventually struggled to his feet and went over to the brow of the hill where he scanned the horizon. As he stood there, he saw it was a burial ground and he looked over the grassland and woods below and feeling the cool wind against his face, he stood there and breathed in deeply. He listened to the silence and found his demons coming slowly under control.

William, Duke of Normandy and William the First of England, was dead. Control of his land in Normandy was given to his eldest son Robert and after his second son was killed in a hunting accident, his third son William known as William Rufus succeeded his father and was crowned king. When he too was killed whilst out hunting, the fourth son quickly claimed the throne and was crowned Henry the First of England.

Henry, like his father, gave large portions of land to his most trusted men buying their support. They in turn gave land to their loyal supporters and the Knight was therefore pleased to accept the hill and its surrounding area as a reward for his services. He managed his land well and built his dwelling on the high ground not far from where the stone cross stood. He was instructed to build a church on the hilltop and the settlement grew around the hill and prospered under his protection.

As the Knight stood staring into the distance, he remembered the Saxon maid he coveted and took to wife, young and fair of face, so delicate, who was soon with child. When her time to be delivered arrived, she struggled through a full day and night and into the next day before the child was born and so weakened by her ordeal, she did not recover. He well remembered the clear morning she was laid to rest on the sheltered side of the hill out of the winds and he took his young son and held him.

The boy grew well in his first years and like his mother was fair of face but when he reached full six years, he was struck down with a sickness in the cold of winter and did not survive. He was buried just below the brow of the hill facing the setting sun and each day the Knight remembered, he stood heavy hearted on the hilltop overlooking where the boy lay.

He eventually took a second wife, an older woman who bore him a strong child, a daughter and although the memory of his son and the young mother who bore him never vanished from his thoughts, he settled and lived his life with his new wife and daughter and was content.

The old Knight suddenly shivered and with his cloak still wrapped tightly around him, he slowly walked with difficulty around the church to the south side where a narrow loop-holed window was set high up in the four foot thick walls of the tower. He stopped to look up at the small carved stone head above the window, a Knight's head to keep watch and it greatly pleased him.

The cold rain beat down steadily as the Knight was laid to rest near, his only son and the men from the settlement silently gathered below the hill to watch. As they slowly

15

went back to their work, each man wondered who would be their new master each feeling uneasy; change always came hard. The Knight's only daughter was soon to wed, would her new husband prove to be a fair master.

The rain stopped and the wind began to blow through the grass, sending it rippling across the hillside as sunlight shone through the clouds and each man who saw it began to feel it was surely a good omen.

Dawn broke and keeping in the shadow of the tower to gain a little shelter from the cold, a thin, wiry figure stood on the hill. He was slightly stooped with continual hard work and his matted grey hair hung each side of his thin face. He stared through the dim light towards the dark shapes of the small dwellings in the distance; he was waiting for his three sons to return so he could join them for the work on the land.

After a stormy night with fierce winds, he had bid his sons to get up and go with him before daylight to collect as many fallen branches as they could find to add to their dwindling woodpile. When they had all the wet branches they could carry, he bid them to go swiftly and take the heavy wood back to the dwelling; he would wait near the hill for them to return. Whilst waiting, he felt the cold bite and decided to climb the hill to the church tower seeking some shelter. Standing there, he suddenly thought of the hill when he was very young before the church with its tower was built.

The hill had always been somewhere quiet; somewhere to go and keep out of the way and he peered through the darkness at the land below and found himself wondering what it would be like living somewhere beyond, away from all he knew. Like many, he could not leave without the master's permission; he was not a 'freeman' he was a serf, a cottar who must work the land, like his father before him.

He suddenly thought of the Knight buried recently on the hillside and remembered standing with his father when all the men were forced to accept what couldn't be altered; now once again, change was upon the village.

The cottar stood on the hill in the quiet of the early morning and knew that whatever happened, they must work the land to eat. He felt the cold wind against his face and shivered. Moving back to stand against the rough, stonewall of the tower, he shuffled his feet and pressed his back harder against the stonework trying to find extra shelter from the cold as he blew on his cupped hands to keep warm. In the dim light, he could just make out a few shadowy figures starting to go about their daily tasks.

The sun slowly appeared breaking through the clouds and he watched the men, young and old, as they made their way slowly past the hill heading towards the land. A few of them called out to each other whilst others silently carried their tools across their shoulders, each man hoping for the sun to warm the ground ready for the spring planting. When his sons came into view, he stretched to ease his aching bones and moved tentatively from the shelter of the tower and headed down the hill to join them.

*

Tom struggled up out of the chair and got his stout walking stick. His knees creaked as he stepped carefully down the couple of shallow steps into the farmhouse scullery and stood a few minutes before going out through the back door. He called to his border collie, Rosie, but there was no sign of her. *Must be with Maggie in the barn*, he thought, *aye, but she'll be with me afore I go through the gate.* And suddenly, there she was at his side.

As he opened the gate leading onto the lane, he stopped to look up at the sky. Although cold, it was a beautiful spring morning and he felt cheerful as he made his way along the familiar route towards the village pond. Calling Rosie to heel, he stopped to watch the ducks waddling in a straight line along the bank, making their way up the lane.

Eventually crossing over the road, he continued towards the snicket, a narrow sloping passageway set between two dry stonewalls, on one side of the passageway stood the village hall surrounded by a neatly cut lawn and on the other sat a row of small cottages with long front gardens. The passageway was easily missed if you didn't know it was there.

Slowly following behind Rosie, who often stopped to see if he was still there, they reached the wrought-iron gate at the top of the snicket that led into the church grounds. Giving it a hefty pull, Tom opened it and continued along the narrow pathway. There in front of him opposite some large yew trees was the old church.

The church itself had stood there since the twelfth century, built by the Normans although much restored and altered over the years. The entrance covered by a modern porch had a wooden bench situated by its side. As Tom made his way past the bench, he stopped to look at the solid looking tower. The walls were reputed to be four foot thick at the base and he looked up at the narrow window with the small carved head above it. He stared intently, it always reminded him of a Knight's head and he nodded good-day as he always did as if greeting an old friend.

Tom followed his usual morning ritual stopping to lean on his stick every so often to get his breath and to enjoy the sight of the remaining snowdrops growing in clumps around the gravestones. Feeling in a good mood as spring was just around the corner, he plodded on past the tower heading for the brow of the hill. Although he found it difficult walking on the grass, he eventually stood where he wanted to be, in front of the tower looking over the scene below.

The impressive Manor Hall built in the early seventeenth century looked as if it would last forever and Tom always felt a sense of pride as he gazed upon it. Everything was familiar to him; he knew every bit of the land surrounding the Manor, stretching out to the horizon.

He looked beyond at the remains of the ancient wood behind the hall where the great yew tree supposedly a thousand years old stood. The trunk so wide, so gnarled and twisted it commanded instant respect. He turned to look at the trees, mainly oaks on the other side of the dry stonewall separating the church ground from the field. They had always been there as far as he could remember and content to be standing on his usual spot with his thoughts the sudden raucous sound of the rooks over in the wood echoed across to the hill and his attention was drawn back to the scene below.

Tom was an old retired tenant farmer in his early nineties and some days he ached all over but today was a reasonably good one, his body just felt tired. He made his way back to the wooden seat near the porch and sat down thankfully to rest beneath the loophole window with the carved head above.

He sat contentedly his eyes closed; he was back in their small cottage where long ago he lived with his wife Meg and their first baby, young Owen. The cottage, still there was their first home before they moved into the farmhouse.

His mind flitted from one thought to another, he remembered before the war when his older brother William was alive and the days seemed continually warm and sunny and he always heard the sound of the house martins as he worked in the garden. He would stand and watch as they dived and swooped from the nearby barns, perching on rooftops or overhead wires. Even now, their chattering noise reminded him of those early days although lately there seemed to be far fewer of them.

Eventually, he and Meg moved to Oldfield Farm with its large farmhouse near the hill. Tom had worked on the land all his working life and had always wanted to run his own farm. His chance came and he worked his fields and took care of his livestock well until he retired a few years ago due to age and an advancing arthritic condition.

He had always been a contented man even in retirement but lately found he frequently yearned for the time when he was young and strong. Although his life had been full of hard physical work, up before dawn, out in all weathers often working late into the night. He still longed for those days.

Being a farmhand since he was twelve years old, Tom had a feeling for the land. Unlike his brother, William, he never wanted to work anywhere else, and always knew one day he would have his own farm to run. Meg had thrown herself into being a farmer's wife; working and helping wherever she was needed. He had stood by her in the beginning and she in turn stood steadfastly by him through the years; they were a good team.

As a widower, Tom knew he had a lot to be thankful for, he still lived at home with his daughters, Maggie and Liz. Neither of them had married, Maggie followed in Tom's footsteps and enjoyed working outside on the land; she took care of all the hens they kept, selling the eggs locally even supplying a few small shops in the town and she looked after the remaining sheep kept in the smaller field behind the barn. Liz was a homely soul who loved to cook and look after the house; she took care of all the household chores and helped Maggie sort and box up the eggs for sale. Between the two of them, they managed the farmhouse, the land and Tom very well.

A slight noise caused him to raise his weary eyelids and coming into focus, a figure stood in front of him gently calling his name, he recognised his daughter-in-law, Kath.

"Hello, Tom, you having five minutes?" Like everybody, she always called him affectionately by his first name.

"Aye," he replied and after a pause added. "What're you doing here then, Kath?"

"Seeing to the church flowers, it's my turn this month." A slight shadow crept over her face as she lowered her voice. "And I've been to see our James."

Tom nodded and quickly looked up at her but the moment passed.

"Shall we go stand on the hilltop?" she asked.

She still had a good-looking face with her warm grey eyes and silver curls. She had been married for well over

21

forty years to his son, Owen, who brought her home when she was eighteen to meet him and Meg, two years later they were married. These days, they lived in a large cottage not far from where Tom and Meg first started their married life all those years ago.

He got up on his feet with some difficulty and Rosie anxiously looked up at him, quickly following close behind. He and Kath walked to the brow of the hill and stood there in compatible silence until he noticed the expression on her face as she looked over the fields and he knew what she was thinking of.

"You okay, Kath?" he said quietly.

"Not really, not today," she answered adding, "but I always feel better just standing here."

And he nodded.

Kath and Owen's youngest daughter, Jen, was a nurse working in a large hospital in London but Tom was always relieved their oldest daughter Laura lived not far away down in the town with her husband, Ben, and their two young boys, Mark and Alex, who were the apple of their grandparent's eye.

He suddenly felt cold and shivered and Kath quickly offered to escort him home. At the backdoor of the farmhouse, Tom turned and unsteadily waved his stick goodbye and Kath waving back suddenly felt a slight pang as she called, "See you soon," adding gently.

"Take care, Tom."

Once inside the scullery, Rosie headed into the kitchen whilst Tom stood at the scullery door looking around the yard for Jess. He peered under the old tree standing there but there was no sign of the younger sheepdog. *Must be with*

Maggie, he thought and a sharp wind suddenly blew across the yard between the barn and the outbuildings causing him to quickly shut the back door.

Feeling the cold seep into his bones, he hurriedly made his way towards the warmth coming from the kitchen ignoring the clutter of old, muddy shoes, boots and wellingtons; he even ignored the half sack of potatoes sitting dejectedly in the corner with the remains of a string of onions hanging on a hook above. Liz was nowhere to be seen so he continued to his own room thankful for the warmth of his fire which Liz always kept banked up for him.

Tom's world had shrunk over the last few years; it now revolved around his room downstairs, his daily walks to the hill and the wooden bench by the backdoor where he would sit if the weather was fine. He would look at his large vegetable plot, remembering when he tended it lovingly and it was full of leeks, onions, cabbages and potatoes. These days, he was lucky to have Owen or Maggie put in a few potatoes and onions.

He no longer went upstairs in the farmhouse and the back parlour was now his domain. It was a cheerful room with his bed in one corner, his favourite armchair sat by the open fire. A round wooden table stood next to his chair with an old-fashioned radio on it and a pile of gardening magazines collected over the months. Although his eyesight was not very good even with his reading glasses on, he still enjoyed a few colourful gardening magazines and seed catalogues to look at.

On the opposite side of the fireplace stood the television, more off than on and above the fireplace on the mantle shelf amongst his treasured family photographs sat an old chiming clock once belonging to William, where William got it from he couldn't remember but it was now one of his own prized possessions. Tom did not need anything else to make his life comfortable and for most of the time, he was pretty content.

The warmth from the fire made him drowsy and he was soon up on the hill. He had just been told the news, he could rent 'Oldfield farm' and move in as soon as they were ready. Meg was expecting Maggie at that time and the cottage they were in already seemed too small with two-year-old Owen toddling around, the farmhouse would be much bigger. He remembered rushing to get home to tell her. He suddenly opened his eyes not knowing where he was but soon pulling himself together, he sat staring at the fire wondering where all the years had gone.

The following morning, Tom leant heavily on his stick as he stood in front of the fireplace enjoying the heat thinking about going out for his usual walk. It had been raining earlier but the sky looked as if was clearing. He noticed his reflection in the large oval mirror above the mantle shelf, a lined weather beaten face with thin iron grey hair swept straight back looked out at him from slightly red rimmed eyes. He refused to wear his glasses unless he was reading and blinking hard, he tried to get a clearer view of himself in the mirror but gave up muttering under his breath as he headed towards the door.

Rosie and Jess were lying in front of the kitchen wood stove and Rosie immediately looked up as Tom entered the kitchen and went straight to his side wagging her tail knowing his morning routine. It was later than he thought and Maggie and Liz were already sitting at the kitchen table with a midmorning brew. They were strong looking women with plump apple cheeks and big smiles like their mother although it was his always his son Owen who reminded him of Meg, he had the same eyes and was blessed with her thick hair. Although these days Owen's hair was silver, if you looked closely you could see glints of his mother's glorious red and gold hair colour.

The two women greeted Tom cheerily and he sat down with them for a few minutes before putting his boots on. Maggie eventually got up ready to return to the barn followed by Jess.

"See you later," she called, giving him a warm smile.

Liz soon wandered upstairs to get on with what she was doing and Rosie looked up expectantly at Tom waiting patiently for him to put his boots on ready to go out for their walk. "Right let's go, Rosie." And Tom heaved himself up with the aid of his stick.

Standing by the back door, he took a deep breath enjoying the smell of the wet grass as he stared at the familiar looking scene in front of him. The chickens clucked and squawked as they ventured out into the sodden yard daintily picking up their feet over the mud whilst his beat up old tractor, the one Maggie used on various occasions sat by the barn like a piece of old furniture. Nothing had changed. It all looked exactly the same, he thought before calling. "Maggie! Are you there?"

"Coming in a minute, why don't you go for your walk before it rains again," she shouted back.

When she came out of the barn, Tom was slowly and carefully going down the lane followed by Rosie plodding along behind him. They were heading for the narrow passageway leading up to the church and the hill.

II

The land baron stopped to look up at the sky before striding around the church tower just as the sun burst through the heavy clouds lighting up the scene before him. He felt the sun's warmth begin to penetrate through his clothing as he continued on his way around the tower. He stood silently beneath the narrow loop-holed window found between two of the buttresses added to the tower for extra support long before his time. He watched the line of men standing opposite the doorway each with a longbow quietly waiting their turn.

King Edward the Third, grandson of Philip the Fourth of France claimed he was not only King of England but also the rightful heir to the French throne; war had been inevitable. His son Edward of Woodstock, known as the Black Prince had already led his father's army the previous year to victory in the battle Crécy and now the King was trying hard to gather together as many new bowmen as possible to replenish the fighting force.

Adding to King Edward's many problems was the plague; it had reached England bringing its dreaded black boils, fever and death. The death toll was so high throughout the land that men were in short supply. Many villages and settlements had been permanently abandoned and Edward's soldiers were sent to collect the chosen bowmen from any village where men had survived.

Following the King's orders, the Land Baron had organised all able bodied men to have a long-bow, kept ready for use, making sure they all attended longbow practise each week. Today the King's soldiers were ready waiting and he knew it was now out of his hands.

Standing in the corner of a buttress and the tower wall where it felt warmer, he continued to watch as a very young but strong looking youth stood ready with his longbow a little apart from the older bowmen and at a signal, the boy placed his arrow into the bow and effortlessly drew it back holding his breath. Letting it go, the arrow whined as it cut through the air just hitting the centre spot of the target.

The boy quickly moved to sharpen his second arrow on one of the stone pillars standing each side of the church door. Fitting it into the bow, concentrating, he pulled it back with strength and once more holding his breath let the second arrow go. It flew straight to the target and this time cleanly hit the centre with a thud and the land baron knew the boy would be counted and taken.

His face impassive, he watched the chosen men standing in line with their longbows, ready to set off with their armed escort and he thought of his own sons already gone to join in the conflict. He had warned them beforehand knowing full well what lay ahead but as always, the young never heed old men's words. When he had seen enough, he turned abruptly and strode off passing the young bowman's father who stood stony faced with the other men.

On the brow of the hill, he stopped to look over the land below as heavy clouds ominously rolling in across the sky covering the sun and he remembered the day he rode into battle for the first time. He could still hear the deafening noise of war, feel the waves of fear, excitement and bloodlust, followed by revulsion of the kill. He remembered the thrill of victory and later the heavy, sick feeling of loathing looking over the battlefield at so many butchered men, some lifeless others still alive but unrecognisable, some begging for the mercy killing.

The many scars on his body from old wounds told their own story and reflecting on the past, he knew well that much blood had been spilt over the years, all to no avail and he closed his eyes for a moment to shut it out of his mind. He stood for some time on the brow of the hill until he felt a calmness of mind and he looked over his familiar land below and was ready to get on with the day.

The cottar knew the outcome as soon as he saw how true his son's aim was, the boy would be sent to join the others and he stood watching, his jaw set tight. Edward's soldiers were ready to escort the chosen men away and he wondered how to manage without his oldest son's help. He was already struggling to grow enough grain to pay the tithes and have enough over to survive through the winter. He had children to feed and now the older, strongest boy was to be taken away.

As a peasant, he worked his small amount of land split into strips in the open land. There was never enough grain to last through the winter months; it had to be eked out with anything else he could manage to grow on a tiny piece of ground near his dwelling and like many villagers, he had to forage hard in the woods. At least, they were allowed 'free warren' by their Lord who knew if they were too weak from hunger, they would be no use; he needed men with strength who could work hard, sowing, reaping, ditching, hedge repairing and anything else needed on the demesne land.

This year, the spring planting was late because of the wet, cold weather and the cottar knew their harvest would be poor and now his son was being sent away and clenching his teeth, he shook his head almost in despair. With dark sunken eyes, he watched the reeve standing nearby and swore an oath under his breath. It was the reeve who made sure there was no trouble, no theft or waste. He kept a tight control on all things, reporting to the old bailiff if he suspected anything amiss.

The chosen bowmen were separated from the rest of the men and soon marched away and those remaining drifted into small groups muttering as they walked down the hill together. Heavy hearted the cottar watched his son and the others being led away and wondered if he would see him again. Deciding to stay near the church until the soldiers had gone, he moved towards the brow of the hill to watch the men being marched out of sight. He noticed the heavy clouds above which did not bode well; it was indeed turning into a dark day.

He saw the remaining men standing about below, some of the younger men beginning to make a nuisance of themselves to the women who were watching nearby. Feeling sick at heart, the cottar felt an urge to go into the church to ask for his son's safe return. He glanced at the carved head above the narrow window as he slowly passed the tower, almost as if he was looking for some sort of

29

reassurance, being nervous and uneasy of going inside the church alone.

At the entrance to the church, he stood staring up at the large stone set in the round arch above the door with the strange figures carved on it and nervously ran his hand down over the pillar where his son had sharpened his arrows. Lifting the iron latch of the heavy door, he slowly opened it but it was so dark inside the building his courage failed and looking quickly around to see if anyone was watching, he mouthed a few hasty words of the only prayer he really knew and let the latch go before hastily retreating back to the brow of the hill.

He saw the boy's mother waiting below with the other women, she looked distraught wringing her hands, some of the women clustered around her, trying to console her before she walked slowly towards their younger children, head bowed.

A silence fell over the hill and he began to feel calmer as he stood staring into the distance. He could almost hear the sound of his son's arrow as it cut through the air and then the thud as it hit the centre of the target. His son's aim was true and for a fleeting moment, he experienced a feeling of pride, his son was a chosen man.

*

Easter Sunday arrived and the church was full. Sitting there, Tom couldn't help noticing all the flowers, daffodils and narcissus overflowing from vases and jars, pots of primroses in between adding to the almost overpoweringly sweet perfume in the air. Behind the altar on the narrow shelf, the usual slim brass vases held elegant tulips and on the carved wooden stand near the pulpit sat a large basket of pure white lilies. He thought the village women who arranged the flowers had done a grand job.

The regulars sat in their usual places and as the organ music suddenly swelled and filled the space the congregation noisily stood for the vicar to take his place and they continued to stand for the opening prayers and hymn.

Once seated, Tom looked around at the families packed into the church and spotted his closest friend, Nell, she was sitting with her daughter and son-in-law. Tom and Nell had known each other since childhood and were the oldest members of the village and when she saw him, she gave a cheery wave. He noticed his neighbour, Ted, from the cottages across the road sitting with his wife, Mary, and behind them were other families he knew well from around the village.

Tom recognised many of the congregation by sight but these days, there were also a number of faces he didn't recognise. It was inevitable when older tenants passed away or moved near to their families, new younger tenants would took their place, but he noticed there seemed to be fewer families with young children these days.

Life in the village continued in general as it had done for years with many of the old traditions still held onto in one form or another. The church always managed to be full during the various festivals held throughout the year although the regular congregation had slowly dwindled. There was only one mid-morning service a month as they had to share the vicar with other parishes in the area and

Tom went when he felt up to sitting in the old stone building for over an hour.

Tom remembered when he was a boy, Easter was a solemn, serious business, especially Good Friday, and there was no playing or making a noise. He and William had to behave and quietly read or draw unless the family went to visit their grandfather who lived nearby and was housebound. The old man was always very pleased to see them with his smiling eyes and lined face. When he laughed, Tom could see the many gaps in his teeth and watched with fascination as he slurped his tea. William said he must be nearly a hundred years old but Tom always thought he must be far older than that.

All the lads we]re happy when Easter Monday arrived; it was always the day of the egg rolling competition which took place over in the long field where a steep slope was situated at one end. Over the years, the event had somehow disappeared and the rules of the game forgotten but Tom always remembered after they rolled their hard-boiled eggs down the slope they excitedly tried to roll themselves down the same slope, over and over again. It was a day worth waiting for.

Tom stopped dreaming and looked at the youngest members of his family sitting in front of him, his granddaughter Laura's boys Mark and Alex. As they sat there, they wriggled and fidgeted as boys do, jabbing each other with their elbows. He was just about to prod them sternly and tell them to sit still when he remembered how the sermon seemed so long when you were young, going on for hours and hours, never ending, he relented and just whispered, "Quiet, lads."

Eventually, the service came to an end and the congregation stood for the last hymn, everyone singing with renewed gusto their voices filling the church and they remained standing for the closing prayers.

After the service when everyone had gone home, Tom sat on his usual bench by the porch, his hands resting on his stick as he waited for Owen and Kath to return from putting flowers on the family graves. After a short while, he became restless and heaving himself onto his feet, he wandered into the porch where he stood staring at the round arched doorway.

He looked up at the ancient semi-circular stone above the door and could just make out the outlines of the simple childlike figures drawn on a chequered background. The stone was said to be much older than the church itself, taken from an earlier site and added by whoever built it.

He stepped closer and ran his hand over the side pillars to feel the wear and tear on them just as he and William had done a thousand times when they were boys. He could hear his father's deep voice telling them the story of the English bowmen, although they had heard it many times and knew it off by heart how the King needed longbow men to fight in his war with France and all men young and old throughout the land were made to practise with the longbow to replenish the army. The bowmen stood near the doorway when practising and sharpened their arrows on the pillars.

Tom and William with the other lads often played at being 'Bowmen of England' or perhaps it was 'Robin Hood'. He couldn't remember but saw himself running around the hill on a warm evening with his homemade bow and arrows. They all spent hours making their bows and

33

each of them tried hard to find the best, most flexible, thin twiggy branches to make them out of. Sometimes they attached bird or chicken feathers to the ends of their arrows but no matter how they made them, they only managed to fly a few feet and land pathetically in the grass. Smiling to himself, Tom thought maybe it was just as well.

William was always the leader of the gang; being a tall, good-looking lad and devil-may care. He was always getting them into hot water but like the others, Tom would loyally follow where his older brother led even if on occasions he was doubtful and it was soon apparent Nell was completely smitten by him.

Tom was more down to earth; he wanted to know how many men were sent off to fight and did they ever come back. He didn't like the idea of being made to leave the village whereas William thought it was all very exciting, an adventure, something he would love to do, march off from the village.

Tom could almost smell those evenings that seemed to go on and on forever. He remembered nostalgically how they whooped and shouted, chasing each other around the church hiding behind the gravestones or the yew trees until it started to get dark when a distant voice of an irate parent could be heard shouting for them to come home for bed. Or else!

Taking a deep breath, he stood staring at the pillars; he could almost hear the sound of an arrow and see the sun glinting off it as it flew through the air. He blinked and staggered a little and just at that moment, Owen and Kath came down the path and saw the old man standing unsteadily by the doorway.

"Are you all right then, Tom, are you ready?" Kath looked at him with a slightly worried look.

"Aye," he answered steadying himself once more with his stick before the three of them headed slowly towards the side gate.

The next morning, feeling in good spirits, Tom followed by Rosie took his usual route to the hill. It was a beautiful day with a clear blue sky as always he enjoyed the spring morning. As he walked contentedly past the soft grey gravestones, he noticed the remaining daffodils looking bright and cheerful, there were a few primroses and the odd cowslip here and there and they always reminded him of his Meg, they were amongst her favourites.

Standing near the tower to catch his breath, he looked at the impressive old walls; it was said they were four foot thick at the base and he read somewhere the heavy buttresses were added a hundred years later, he couldn't remember why but they always looked to him as if they were propping the tower up. He looked up at the carved head above the narrow window, it stared straight ahead as usual and he gave it a quick nod as if to say 'good morning'.

As it was a fine day, he decided to try and venture a further around the tower to the north side of the church, it was such a long time since he had tried to walk around there and even longer since he had managed to actually get to the stonewall separating the church from the adjoining field. There used to be horses standing beneath the shelter of the oak trees but he hadn't seen any for some time. He suddenly spotted something he had totally forgotten, a large moss covered stone barely visible in the thick grass.

Tom knew what it was and taking his time, he struggled over to have a better look. The large worn stone had a square hole in the centre and was said to be the base of a Saxon Cross, much older than the church itself although the shaft had vanished long before Tom's day. As he stood staring at the ancient stone, it suddenly stirred some distant memories.

When he and Nell were young, they often sat on the stone base, sheltered by the wall talking, arguing as they waited for William and the others to join them. Nell had a sharp sense of humour and she always entertained him with her antics, continually up to some scheme or other, full of energy.

He suddenly remembered the day they sat there and he indulged himself in a few passionate thoughts about Nell and tried to steal a kiss or two but she pushed him off balance and he fell off the stone into a clump of nettles that stung him painfully. He jumped up ready to shout at her when he heard her whisper, "Sorry, Tom," and she took his hand and he instantly forgave her.

He knew full well Nell considered herself vastly superior in age being in the class above him in school and her head was already full of William but undeterred, he thought he would just try his luck. He had to practise somewhere and Nell was his best friend, she would do; surely, she wouldn't mind.

It was Nell who eventually introduced him to her younger friend Meg, who had moved into the village with her parents from distant Wales and like herself was an only child. Meg was completely opposite to Nell, not only in looks but by nature. She was shorter and fuller in figure than Nell and always looked serious, even a little forbidding until she smiled. It completely transformed her face from being rather plain into something akin to beauty. Her lovely thick hair was her crowning glory and Tom found himself rather attracted to her although Nell continued to hover somewhere in the back of his mind.

Memories of warm evenings filled his head. When he was older, he and Meg would sometimes loiter on the hill after church in the evening enjoying being alone. He liked to talk to her and they often stood or sat if it was dry on the grass near the base of the cross leaning against the dry stonewall. He could hear himself telling her the plans he had. He wanted to rent his own farm from the estate, grow his crops and eventually have a small flock of sheep; she would listen and nod with approval.

Nell was still there in Tom's thoughts until one evening everything changed. It was warm, work was done and after his dinner, he went out for a walk and saw Meg standing near the yew trees opposite the church. She had been to see a friend and taken a shortcut home. They strolled together past the porch, around the tower, stopping to stand on the brow of the hill as the sun began to set. Without thinking, deep in conversation, he took her hand and they continued to the usual spot watching the changing colours of the evening sky before sitting down for a few moments by the wall.

Tom looked at Meg and saw the shape of her creamy white neck as she bent forward to look at some small plant or object she'd noticed in the grass. He looked at the thick golden red hair piled up on top of her head and saw the feminine curves hidden by the folds of her dress and she looked up at him with eyes wide open and in that moment, they were overcome by the nearness of each other. They were both powerless, passion and nature took its course.

The day soon came when Meg with a pale drawn face met him by the church and he guessed what she was going to tell him. As they stood sheltered from the wind between the two heavy buttresses there on the hill, he had to grow up and face his responsibilities. It had shocked him although deep down, he had instinctively known and being a loyal, honourable man, he and Meg were wed soon afterwards and any remaining thoughts of Nell were put aside.

Suddenly feeling tired, Tom looked around to see where Rosie was and he struggled through the grass back to the tower and stood with Rosie close by his side. A slight breeze rippled through the grass as the sun shone and suddenly he remembered it was Easter Monday and the old saying how the sun danced for joy on Easter Monday and if you climbed a hill high enough, you could see it and he automatically turned to have a look.

On the way home, Tom noticed Ted had made a start digging and turning the soil over in his garden ready to plant a few early crops. Ted and Mary lived opposite Tom in the row of small cottages next to the passageway leading to the church grounds. He was younger than Tom by eight years which made him a mere eighty four, almost a youngster in Tom's eyes. They had been neighbours for years and always in the past competed against each other in the village show.

These days, Tom couldn't dig his own garden due to the arthritic condition of his once large frame. His age and years of continual manual work in all weathers had taken its toll and now he had to rely on Owen to do any serious digging and Maggie to help him with the planting if she had time.

His poor garden was sadly neglected and often left to its own devices but he always had a few potatoes or onions in and he was grateful for that. He made his way home as quickly as he could to ring Owen to tell him Ted had already made a start on his spring garden.

That evening, Owen with Nell's son-in-law John walked down to Tom for a game of dominoes. It was a lovely clear night and they fancied the walk.

"How's things, John?" Tom asked. "I've not seen you to for a chat lately."

John was married to Nell's only daughter Tess and the two families had been close friends for many years.

"Not bad, Tom, thanks, I've been pretty busy lately," was the reply.

Soon the only sound in the kitchen was the shuffling of dominoes as the game started in earnest. After a game or two, it was time to call it a night. Tom who usually beat them was feeling tired. His mind was far away that evening but he playfully said he let them win deliberately to give them a chance.

The two younger men made their way from the kitchen to the back door in the scullery and Rosie who was asleep by Tom's feet lifted her head as they opened the door latch but settled back down as they shouted goodnight.

Owen called to his father as he and John stepped out into the cold air.

"There'll be a frost tonight, Tom, it feels pretty sharp; stay in and keep warm."

"Aye, I will," Tom replied. "Goodnight both."

Getting up from the table before he returned to his room, Tom looked through the kitchen window and saw how clear the night sky was with a bright moon lighting up the trees and he could even see a few of the larger stars. It made him feel happy. He could almost smell the cold air and it brought back those distant days of boyhood.

Once in bed, Tom pulled his blankets up under his chin, glad to see the glow from the fire, Liz had banked it up for him. He closed his eyes and could hear the owl, an old friend, gently hooting in the distance and he fancied he saw moving figures running around the church. He heard the clear voices of William and the others as they called out the secret password clutching their homemade bows and arrows, chasing each other in the moonlight. He remembered thinking they were the real 'Bowmen of England' just like years ago and suddenly he was with them underneath the clear, starlit sky, young and carefree, full of life. He could hear the sound of laughter and the noise as they continued to chase each other around the church up on top of the hill.

*

III

Walking past the stone cross deep in thought with her maid following behind at a discreet distance. She stopped on the hilltop where she spent much of her time during many long weeks, looking over to the horizon, waiting, watching for the sight of her husband. The mistress had been very pleased to see him return home safely before the winter solstice, ready to take up his duties and she prayed there would be no more wars so he would stay.

King Henry the Fifth of the House of Lancaster had ruthlessly defeated the French at Agincourt and returned to England triumphantly with his men to be cheered by the crowds thronging the decorated streets of London. Eventually, the surviving knights and barons with their men wearily returned to their lands and families, glad to be home from the war where they fought alongside the King.

Although no longer young, the mistress was still in her prime and deemed a great beauty by all who looked upon her. She had married when very young and although the land had been her inheritance, like her grandmother and great, grandmother once she married, her husband took control as lord and master and she accepted the fact and was content.

She stood quietly on the hill and felt the breeze blowing gently around her delicate neck and quickly pulled the hood of her cloak up over her head. It was now late spring and she found she was once more with child and was on her way to offer her daily prayers in the church, to give thanks and ask for God's mercy. Sadly, she lost her first born at birth, a boy and later a little girl a beautiful child who succumbed to the fever in her second year and the thought of losing this new baby was unbearable. This one must be kept safe, strong and healthy.

Leaving the peaceful interior of the dimly lit church, she sent her maid back to the dwelling to wait for her saying she would return shortly. She wanted time alone to think, she must plan.

The maid left her as instructed, glancing back nervously worried in case master was not pleased her mistress was being left on her own. She had been with her for many years, even before mistress was wed, she knew her moods well and was anxious now she was once more in a delicate condition. Passing the Saxon Cross, she stopped and gently touched the cold, rough stone whispering a prayer under her breath before hurrying on.

The mistress stood near the arched doorway of the church after visiting the small graves of her children who lay on the south side of the hill, sheltered from the wind; she shut her eyes and remembered the many tears she shed after the loss of each child. They were buried where the land dipped away creating a slight hollow that seemed to cradle them. She had grieved pitifully after them, especially the sweet and tender little girl whose life was so brief. She grieved so much she had been confined to her bed taking time to recover and regain her strength.

She suddenly noticed the carved head above the narrow window and stood quietly staring at it for a few moments; she liked to think it was perhaps watching over her children. Going to stand on the brow of the hill, she stood there quietly thinking of the new life inside her giving her feelings of new hope. Although excited, she wanted to hold her breath lest she disturb the child, she must do something to help, to give this baby a chance. She knew her husband must have an heir and she desperately wanted to bear a son for him who would survive and grow strong to inherit the land.

As she stood there, she suddenly noticed the elderly cottar working below and recognised him immediately, he was one of her maid's family. Unsteady on his feet with poor eyesight, he no longer toiled from dawn to dusk leaving his grown sons to grow the grain needed for the family to survive. He now worked doing any odd job he was told needed doing but his skill was planting and growing young trees. They all said he had a special gift.

He was standing near the spring well situated below where water constantly bubbled from the ground and she saw him lift some fresh cut yew branches off a small wooden handcart and lay them by the well ready. She suddenly remembered this was the time of year when they blessed the wells and the villagers gave thanks for their good source of water. The women used the new spring growth taken from yew trees to decorate the wells combining it with as many wild flowers as they could find, weaving them amongst the greenery.

She remembered the large ancient yew that stood in the wood and an idea began to form in her mind. There were many whispered stories surrounding the old tree, some said it had been there forever and had mystical qualities. Yews lived longer than other trees and she had heard the stories of them called 'trees of life and death', a symbol of everlasting life, some said they kept evil away and purified the ground, this made her think, there were two young yews growing behind the church but more planted near the church doorway taken from the ancient yew would indeed be special.

She beckoned to the worker who dutifully climbed the hill with some difficulty to see what his Mistress wanted. She knew he helped with the planting of young trees and she asked him to find a couple of saplings grown from the old yew. He must plant them opposite the church door where she would make sure they were looked after well and they would grow sturdy and strong. One day when fully grown, they would give shelter to all approaching the door of the Holy Church and after the cottar left to do her bidding she thought surely God would surely see she cared and maybe keep this new child safe.

Her maid came looking for her, the Master wanted to know where she was, she must rest. The Mistress immediately set off but as if drawn to the hilltop she was compelled to stop and give one last look over the land below before dutifully returning to her husband to do his bidding.

The Master was preparing to go down to inspect the men working on the land to see if all was ready for the planting of the spring crops. Although the Mistress understood much of the day-to-day running of the land, she was a little bewildered by some of her husband's ideas. He had seen and heard of many new ways to improve crops and yields and when she gave it some thought, it pleased her. If they had a strong child who would inherit all the land, it surely must be a worthy, profitable inheritance.

She nodded to her husband respectfully as he bade her go and rest. His face reminded her of the carved head above the window in the tower of the church, the same, solemn countenance. He suddenly smiled at her and his face relaxed, she felt safe and retired to her bedchamber as commanded.

The old cottar slowly carried the water up the hill to the saplings, they looked healthy and he was more than satisfied. He had done what mistress wanted. When fully grown, they could be as high as the tower and as he stood looking at them, he wondered would anyone care who planted such fine trees. He looked at the grass around the saplings worn by the many feet treading it down as they headed up to the church door and he thought maybe mistress would ask him to plant a few more each side forming a pathway.

Although strong enough to carry out the work given him each day, his eyes no longer saw clearly and he had to be careful where he trod, he was thankful he could still get about. Walking with difficulty around the tower using the rough blocks of stone to steady himself, he stood between the buttresses on the front looking out as far as he could see. It was warm and the sky was heavy with clouds and he knew it would soon rain. He stood looking over the land below and could just make out men toiling in the distance, working on the land and he remembered when he was young and strong as an ox, able to do the work of two men, doing what was needed to survive now his four sons worked the land

and he just did whatever the master or mistress asked him to do.

It felt good just standing on the hilltop looking over the land and he stood there some time in the quiet for no one else was around and the stillness surrounded him and he was content until eventually he stirred himself and set off unsteadily down the hill.

*

The month of May began with never ending wet weather until one morning the sun shone in a clear sky and the house martins magically appeared. They perched on the overhead wires, making their familiar chattering noise, darting from one perch to another with lightning speed and splendid aerobatic displays. Tom stopped to watch them before he went to find Maggie feeling his old friends had returned at last and it made him feel light hearted and cheerful. Everyone knew it was time to start planting in earnest as soon as the house martins appeared, they were the signal; they always turned up when the frosts were over.

"We can make a start now, they're here, Maggie," he shouted.

"You mean I can," she replied a bit waspishly as she stepped out of the barn with Jess following behind her. She looked at Tom and gave him a smile knowing full well she always helped him with his garden.

Tom loved the month of May. The weather was usually warmer, his aching body felt better, everything smelt of spring and shortly it would be Ascension Day, the time for the village to start decorating the wells. The old practise of dressing the wells went back as far as Tom could remember and feeling in good spirits, he decided to call on his pal before going for his walk. He wanted to know what Ted was going to plant in his garden this year.

"I'll come and give you a hand with yours, Tom," offered Ted as they sat enjoying the sun. The seat they were sitting on was situated opposite the duck pond on a small grassy bank just in front of Ted's garden.

"It must be getting a bit much for Maggie these days." Ted continued, "And it's not so easy for your Owen to spare the time after work either."

"Aye okay," replied Tom. "Just a row of earlies will be fine and maybe a row of onions. Don't tell Maggie what you've just said mind, or we'll cop it. You know what women are; they think they can do everything." Ted laughed and nodded.

Tom sat back and thought of his daughters; Maggie had always been strong and independent and just didn't seem to have the time or a need to be married and Liz had been courting some years ago with a young chap, Tom couldn't remember his name, but he accepted a job in a large city up in the north. She refused point blank to go with him so it ended before it really began and since then there had been no one else.

Tom kept forgetting Maggie and Liz were no longer young. Although he still thought of them as 'the girls', they were now in their sixties and like everyone were plain set in their ways. Tom felt more than fortunate and was pleased to live with them; they looked after him so well and suddenly he felt guilty for being stubborn on occasions and a bit cantankerous.

47

The two men continued to sit in silence on the wooden seat, each with their own thoughts. Ted leant back with the sun on his face, his eyes shut and Tom after making a decision to try harder to be patient at home sat contentedly with his hands resting on his stick. Glancing up, he spotted Joe who lived in one of the smaller cottages on the back lane. He just appeared from under the overhanging trees into the sunshine, a stocky figure with hunched shoulders and long, thick unruly hair covering his ears.

"Hello, Joe, you okay?" called Ted suddenly opening his eyes and Tom waved his stick in greeting.

"Yes, thanks," mumbled Joe as he continued on down the lane as if in a hurry.

Both men watched as Joe disappeared and when he had passed out of sight Tom slowly shook his head, the year before Joe had lost his wife in tragic circumstances; she sadly had taken her own life. No one knew the real ins and outs of the whole business but it shocked the village. The couple rented their small cottage on the back lane where Joe still lived. Unfortunately, as far as anyone knew, he had no family to turn to and had been unable to work after the tragedy until he was lately given a part time job at a large farm nearby. Although Joe usually kept himself to himself, he would on occasions pass the time of day with Ted and Tom if he was so inclined.

"Poor chap, if only he talked a bit more," Ted murmured.

"Aye, trouble is, it looks as if he has no one close to talk to," Tom replied.

Eventually, Tom got up calling a cheery goodbye to Ted, it was time to continue his walk and Rosie sprang to her feet following him as he set off carefully turning into the passageway heading for the church gate. He stood a moment savouring the serenity of the grounds before carrying on. As he reached the church door, he decided to sit for a few minutes to catch his breath.

More than happy to sit there opposite the yew trees, Tom suddenly noticed Joe standing beneath one of the yews. Joe didn't answer Tom's greeting; just stood there lost in his own thoughts until suddenly he rapidly set off between the old trees downhill towards the Lane. Tom stared after him and sadly wondered what was going through the poor chap's mind.

As the yews stirred in the breeze, Tom's thoughts were drawn towards them standing majestically each side of the sloping driveway going down to a set of gates. He knew they must be hundreds of years old because of their girth and height and he pondered what the hill would have looked like before they were planted there. He could envisage the grass beneath worn by the many villagers who probably climbed up that sheltered side of the hill to reach the church door creating a pathway.

Rested, he got up and made his way around the tower to stand as usual on the hilltop looking down on the scene in front of him. Noticing the largest of the village wells, he suddenly remembered it would soon be time for the blessing of the wells on Ascension Day. Every year like all the villages in the area, families and neighbours worked together to decorate the wells. Tom and Nell's families always worked on the well up at the top end of the village and used the old barn with the cobbled yard to carry out the task.

He remembered the village men in his younger days preparing the heavy wooden boards they used for the designs before covering them in heavy, wet clay dug from the local stream. One whole day was spent treading the heavy clay, ready to be put on the boards whilst the women went to collect as many fresh wild flowers and greenery they could find to do the work. They used the new spring growth from the yews and buckets full of bluebells from the woodland beside anything else they could find to complete the work. It was the smell of bluebells that reminded Tom of well dressing week. Meg used to say she could smell the scent of bluebells for days afterwards, even when she was nowhere near the old barn.

The wind stirred and Tom decided to go and sit a while on his seat for a few minutes before setting off home. Sheltered from the wind, he sat with his eyes closed, dozing, enjoying a bit of warmth. He could see his Meg hurrying down the hill on her way to meet Nell and the other women to help with the well dressing flowers. He could see her wearing her old tatty fur boots to keep her feet warm. He always used to tease her but she just laughed and said she didn't care what they looked like, they did the job. It suddenly struck him she'd been gone for more than twenty years, so long ago, although sometimes it seemed like yesterday.

"Tom!"

He heard a voice calling his name. Nell was standing in front of him leaning heavily on her stick. "Morning, Tom, you're miles away."

"Aye," he replied.

"Tess is doing the flowers for the church and I came with her."

They sat together fully at ease until Tom muttered, "My legs are getting worse, 'our Nell'?"

"Why, what's the matter with them?" she asked.

"Not much, just old age."

"You're not as old as me, Tom, and at least you can still move them."

He laughed, typical Nell, sharp as a tack with a wicked tongue but somehow she always made him feel alive and he took his old friend's hand and squeezed it.

That night, Tom's knees hurt. "It must be sitting too long with Nell," he muttered under his breath and he rubbed some strong smelling liniment into the offending knees before retiring for the night. Eventually, he fell asleep, but by midnight was wide awake. He tossed and turned and couldn't get comfortable until eventually he got up.

It was pitch black outside and silent but the kitchen wood burner gave out a low heat and felt comforting, Rosie and Jess stirred as he sat down in the old chair in the corner. He sat there in the warmth and Rosie always pleased to see him got up and padded over. She sat down and resting her head on his lap looked up at the careworn face. Jess just opened his eyes and gave a quick wag of his tail before going back to sleep.

"What's the matter, Dad?" Maggie opened the door and poked her head around. "Are you all right?"

"Just aching; go back to bed and don't fuss." He snapped and feeling sorry for his bad attitude tried to give her a bit of a smile.

"Here take this," adding, "I bet Nell's the same. Serves you two right sitting so long, neither of you listen."

"Nell's too old to listen, she's ninety four," he grunted.

"Aye and you're ninety-three yourself next month," Maggie replied shaking her head and Tom looked surprised. "I suppose I am."

The well dressing week passed by quickly and the wells were all finished on time for the Ascension Day Blessing and Tom began to feel hopeful the village would be back to peace and quiet with the many visitors going home where they came from.

The following week meandered along with some fine weather and one morning, Tom set off for his walk to the hill. It was early and he could hear the sound of the lambs over in the fields bleating for the ewes in the clear morning air. He passed through the side gate following the winding path and stopped near the yews and on a whim stumbled through the layers of dried, dead foliage struggling to get as close to the trees as he could, he felt an urge to touch the rough old textured bark.

He remembered how sometimes they played around the tree trunks as youngsters and even stuck secret messages on bits of paper into the crevices of the bark. Although the yews were not as ancient as the big yew down in the wood with its heavy branches these days propped up with supports, they were still old enough to command some respect.

He stood beneath the dark green branches that swayed gently back and fore in the breeze, listening to their sound and remembered the whispers of the beautiful woman who stood beneath the yews early in the morning before walking towards the carved head of the knight. It was said many were scared to go alone to the church grounds first thing but Tom had never seen anything and he wondered where that particular story came from. He stood for a few moments running his hand once more over the textured bark before struggling to get back on the narrow path.

He sat resting for a while on his seat, getting his breath back, when he suddenly wished Nell were there to keep him company. They could have reminisced together and giving a sigh. He decided it was time to make his way home. As he stood up his knees and legs began to ache and he painfully made his way to the side gate heading down the narrow passageway to the lane. It took him much longer than usual to get home and even with his walking stick, he was very unsteady on his feet. Relieved to reach the back door of the farm and thankfully staggered into the house.

Later that week feeling a bit stronger, Tom made his way down the lane with Rosie and found Ted busy in his front garden. They were just chatting about the state of the soil when Owen turned up in his old working truck and brought a large cardboard box out from the back.

"What've you got there, Owen?" asked Ted.

At that moment, Joe appeared and Tom called him to come over to join them; after hesitating Joe did. They all stood peering inside the box. It contained a number of healthy looking plants.

"I've just been given these, thought you might be interested," said Owen with a grin and Tom recognised them immediately.

"Look at those beauties, Owen," he said. "Marrow plants, the long trailing variety. You know the sort that needs plenty of room and gallons of water."

Tom sighed and shook his head. "I daren't ask Maggie to see to them, she's enough to do already."

"I'll have some," answered Ted quickly.

"What about you Joe do you want any?" asked Owen.

"I've nowhere to plant them," Joe replied. "I'd like some but my bit of front garden is full of bushes and established shrubs and I've no back garden." He seemed a bit crestfallen.

"Plant them in mine if you want to, Joe, I've plenty of room," said Tom. "Maybe we can have a few plants each; I'd like to see them growing there for old time's sake."

After thinking for a few moments, Joe nodded. "Okay!" He hesitated. "I could look after them if you like and I'll plant them in after work tomorrow."

"Aye, we can be partners," Tom answered and Joe almost gave him a bit of a smile. Ted became enthusiastic "We could even enter them in the show this year, just like we used to." And Tom nodded his eyes brightening. Owen left the plants with Ted and he and Joe went their separate ways.

Tom lingered a while, talking about the old days with Ted before he set off home but as he stepped through the gateway into the farmyard not concentrating where he was going he put his foot down on a patch of uneven gravelled ground and fell. Luckily, he hung onto the open gate and saved himself from falling heavily although he still went down on his knees and Rosie started to bark. Ted who saw what happened from his front garden hurried over.

"Hang on, Tom, I'm coming."

He picked up Tom's stick from where he dropped it and with some difficulty helped him to stand upright and gave him his stick. Slowly, they staggered into the kitchen and Ted managed to sit him down. They were both out of breath.

"Are you there, Liz?" Ted called and she came hurrying downstairs.

"I'm all right, I'm all right." Tom began to feel irritated by the attention. "Just help me to my room and I'll put my feet up. No doctor. Okay." He was adamant.

There was no arguing and they helped him to his room and as he put his feet up on his stool she tried to soothe him, to sound unconcerned and with a bit of a laugh she told him if Maggie were there, she'd be telling him off.

"I know, I know." He snapped and Rosie who was standing quietly at the side of him raised her head quickly to look at him. Liz frowned and thanking Ted for his help bid him to sit down awhile and she hurried to get them both a drop of brandy to steady their nerves.

Tom sat in his chair feeling rattled and when Liz and Ted eventually left him to it, he softly muttered, "Bugger and damnation!" He rarely swore but was so upset by his own carelessness he let go for a few minutes relieving his frustration.

After much persuading, Liz and Maggie got him to see the doctor who told him to rest a few days with his feet up. Tom laid his head against the cushion at the back of his chair and although fed up he was resigned to do as he was told and soon drifted off by the fire until Rosie nudged his arm wanting him to stroke her head.

Once awake, he tried hard to keep his mind off his fall thinking of young Joe. Would he really come and work in the garden like he said he would? Tom wanted to see a few marrows growing like the old days and with his eyes closed, he could see the lovely plants filling his old veg plot.

Eventually, Tom's thoughts turned to his Meg, how he wished she were still here with him. He suddenly felt lonely and his spirits fell until Nell who always cheered him up popped into his mind, these days he missed her when she wasn't about. He remembered what a fine looking girl she was, high spirited and completely drawn to William with his good looks. They were always together, everyone thought of them as a couple but later on things went wrong and they seriously fell out. William and Nell refused to talk about it and ignored each other completely afterwards. Tom often wondered what really happened.

William went out with one or two girls after Nell but there was no one special and not long after the war broke out, he was one of the first in the village to join up. When he was sent home from France after being badly wounded, Nell rushed to go to him, their quarrel forgotten but William never recovered from his war time ordeal and was left with permanent scars to body and mind. He died just before the war ended and Tom remembered how Nell took it so badly and refused to talk about it to anyone.

Later, she went to work on the large farm further up the valley run by their old friend Jack from school days who was a bit older, he always wanted Nell and patiently waited. Eventually, the two of them settled down together and soon were happily married.

Opening his eyes, Tom saw the fire burning brightly, Rosie was lying stretched out in front of it and she looked up at him wagging her tail and Tom felt his spirits lifting. He remembered about Joe and enthusiastically called Liz to see if she could find his old gardening manuals. He was sure Joe would come and plant the marrows when he had the time.

"It will be like the old days, Rosie," he said out loud and she got up and sat in front of him. Tom stroked her head suddenly content. He would soon be up and about going for his walk, sitting on his favourite seat watching the old yews as they swayed gently back and fore.

*

IV

As dawn broke, the Lord of the Manor bid his men to wait for his return, he was going to check the chosen site for his new dwelling and he wanted to look from the vantage point on the hill. He stood in front of the church tower and looked over the ground below where it was going to be built. It would be a strong stone building, square in shape and he knew exactly where he would build it, he knew even as a young man before he inherited the land.

Hidden away in his mind lay hidden fears, images of wooden cottages burning filled him with feelings of dread. The details of the fires were not clear to him but he vaguely remembered when a very young child the terrifying sight of large flames reaching up into the sky which frightened him. He could still hear the sounds and screams of women and children as they watched, he could see villagers rushing around and men shouting to each other, unable to control the blaze. The years passed by and although now much older he was left with a dread of fire and it haunted him still. His new dwelling would be built, not of wood but of solid stone.

When Elizabeth the First was crowned, all the barons and knights pledged their loyalty to the new queen. She had reigned for forty years becoming queen after the death of her half-sister Mary. Through the years, she had to deal with religion, intrigues, rebellions and wars and although she was a woman she claimed she was as brave as any man. She had learnt to contend with all the problems that went with the crown. However, she took no husband and the future looked very uncertain now she was old and there were no children to follow in her footsteps.

When Henry the Eighth declared himself, head of the Church in England after his split with Rome, the village around the hill, like all villages had to accept the changes imposed on them. Likewise when Mary, Henry's oldest daughter by Catherine of Aragon, a devout catholic was eventually crowned, the village had to revert hurriedly back to Catholicism, to do otherwise was not an option.

The old men and women of the village whispered the name of Mary for years; they well remembered being told stories about threats of execution by burning alive. Protestants who would not give up their beliefs were called heretics and punished by death; it filled the cottars with fear and dread. The new young queen had been more than welcomed.

The master continued to stand on the hill and felt satisfied for his men had already carried out his instructions for the church. He had given orders for them to erect a newly carved altar rail. It was made of strong oak with turned pillars, the sections carved by his chosen master craftsmen in the town some distance away. The new rails was partly to please his wife; a godly woman of strong character and now it had been erected in the church, tomorrow he would take her to see it, pleasing her immensely.

He reconsidered the possibility of having a wooden gallery built at the back of the church. His wife had already made it known to him one of her wishes was for there to be more room for the faithful servants to attend the services. He considered steps being built up the outside of the south wall leading to a window that could be used as a doorway into the gallery; with careful planning, he knew it could be done.

He suddenly thought of the carved head above the loophole window in the tower. For years, he had studied the stone head and wondered who it was, there were many guesses but no one seemed to really know for sure. Was it someone who once owned the land or built the church? No one knew; he would make sure this would not happen to him. He already had a large family memorial being carved, to be erected when finished. It comforted him to think in years to come his family would be truly remembered. He had carefully given detailed instructions to his son to make sure the work was completed as he wished it. The memorial would have a large inscription and everyone would see and know the family name. They would not be forgotten and he was more than satisfied and content with all his plans as he walked back to his men who were patiently waiting his return.

The cottar waited until he saw the Master return to his waiting men and then quickly headed up to the church and stood against the solid stone tower trying to keep in the shadows between the buttresses. He stood sullenly looking down over the scene below, his sour look showed how he felt.

His chosen woman had refused him as her husband and he felt bitter. He always had her in mind whilst he struggled to gain the right to work a larger portion of land; thinking if he increased his grain yield, it would help to provide for a wife and her father would look favourably on him. A beauty to look upon he had always wanted her and taken it for granted his offer would be accepted. Instead, he was told she was already promised to someone else. She told him she had to obey her father's wishes and must please her family. They exchanged harsh words and for days, he held strong feelings of anger towards her and her family.

He thought of the times he called to her as she passed by when he was working in the fields and she would smile and wave and linger with him a while. Why did she dally with him, encourage him, if she did not want him and was promised to another. For a moment, he felt more than bitter, his anger rising once again. He remembered the many times on his way back to his dwelling after a long day's work he would go up on the hill to think of ways to please her. Working hard each day, the time had passed by too quickly and now she was promised to another, why didn't she tell him?

Whatever his grievance was, the cottar kept it to himself for he knew well to provoke the men in charge was to create problems and for anyone who caused deliberate problems there were penalties inflicted. Their master although a fair man did not usually interfere in what he considered the smaller matters amongst the villagers and left his bailiff to take care of the day-to-day running of things.

He watched as the blacksmith's daughter slowly plodded up the hill. She was plain and solid looking and he knew her well. She made her way past the tower as she did most days to take food for her younger brother tending sheep over in the distant meadow. She saw him standing there by the tower and waved as she went by and he raised his hand in greeting.

Cold rain had continued on and off for weeks and they were all waiting hopefully for some sign of better weather. As he stood looking down on the sodden fields below his eyes were suddenly drawn to the smoke rising from the cottages clustered together. He thought of his brother already settled with a wife and small son. The years had passed quickly and he knew it was more than time for him to take a wife and start a family of his own.

The sound of men going about their daily tasks nearby disturbed his thoughts and he looked over towards the Master's large dwelling which had seen better days. The timbers were beginning to rot in places and everyone had heard he was going to build a fine new building to replace it. It would be a large stone structure opposite from where he stood. It was rumoured it would have large windows and tall chimneys and on the inside, there would even be carved wooden panels. They said it would be the finest dwelling in the area and many servants would be needed to look after it and he turned away feeling resentful.

He stood on the hilltop with the wind blowing around him and slowly it started to soothe his inner spirit. He stood listening to the branches of the yew trees swishing back and fore until he saw dark, clouds spreading quickly across the sky towards the church and he heard a rumble overhead. A loud crash made him jump and the sound echoed around the hill, large drops of water started to fall and he decided to run and seek shelter under the trees.

As he passed the tower, his eyes were drawn to the solemn stone head above the narrow window but the rain increased and he hurried on by to get out of it. He stood under the branches of the yews opposite the church door until a bolt of lightning shot to earth and he wondered if it was punishment for his anger and he felt fearful. It would surely be a safer place inside the church and scared he ran as fast as he could towards the doorway.

Once accustomed to the dark, the cottar looked towards the chancel arch where a newly carved altar rail had been erected and with the slight apprehension he always felt when he was inside the church he approached the rail reverently. It had only been put in place the day before; he knew for he had seen the rail with the turned pillars loaded up on a horse drawn cart when it arrived in the village. The smell of the newly carved wood mingled with the damp musty odour of the church filling his nostrils. He stepped forward and bravely reached out to touch the wooden rail. The surface felt smooth and he wondered what it would be like to make something from a piece of solid oak or any wood.

He began to feel cold and shivered quickly moving to the back of the church where he stood for a moment trying to peer through the narrow window at the rain. He could only just see the light between the thick stonewalls but felt the wind as it blew coldly through the opening. He quickly moved to the door and went out into the fresh air. The rain was coming down steadily although the thunder had rolled away and making his mind up to get off back to his dwelling he ran down the pathway to the muddy lane below.

Water dripped off him as he pushed his way into the small, cramped smoke filled cottage where the family lived together. His brother sat close to the fire on a wooden bench next to an old man who sat with eyes staring at the glowing embers of the fire continually picking at his ragged clothing. His father muttered and fretted to himself under his breath and he remembered him as a strong working man, now pitiful, thin and pale in contrast to the child asleep on the straw bedding in the corner, his little face flushed and pink.

His brother's wife looked at him as he entered the cottage, she saw he was cold and wet and offered him food from the steaming cooking pot hanging over the fire. He felt comforted and as he noisily ate the food offered to him. He suddenly thought maybe he would go and approach the old blacksmith from the north end of the settlement to ask about his daughter. She was a good hard working girl who always looked favourably upon him, they had played together as children and he knew she would accept his offer and suddenly feeling in a better frame of mind, he sat almost contentedly warming himself by the fire.

*

It rained over the last week of May until eventually by the beginning of June, the sun made a welcome appearance. Tom sat out on his wooden bench by the back door and watched the sparrows congregating around the bird table nearby. He watched the hungry blue-tits and other small birds as they clung to the feeders that were hanging from various branches of the old apple tree. A pair of magpies tried hard to barge in with bully tactics but it was no good, they were too big for the small bird table and not agile enough for the feeders. They had to be content to join the slow moving wood pigeons walking around underneath picking up whatever tasty morsels they could find.

Tom had earlier struggled to his vegetable garden to look at the newly planted marrow plants, they were doing well and Joe, as instructed, had carefully put straw around them, to keep them off the wet earth. Tom remembered. It was the eighth of June and the Oldfield Farming rhyme came to his mind – 'If on the eighth of June it rain, it foretells a wet harvest'.

And as it was a sunny morning, he was pleased. Sitting by the backdoor in a bit of warm sunshine, Tom felt fine but since the day he'd fallen, his confidence had taken a knock. He hadn't tried to go for his usual walk up to the hill but this morning as it was dry and warm he decided to have a go walking down as far as the seat by the pond near Ted's front garden.

It took some effort to get going but he set off concentrating where he put his feet. By the time he reached the pond, his limbs felt weak and he was worn out trying to keep his balance; maybe it wasn't such a bad idea having one of those wheeler contraptions Owen was always on about. At first, he was stubbornly against it but now he realised he had nothing to lose: it was getting harder to get around with just his stick. He began to feel a bit low but at that moment, Ted who was working in his garden popped his head up over the wall and shouted to Tom.

"Hey, Tom, how are the marrows doing? Mine are doing well."

"Not as good as ours," Tom shouted back, struggling to get up.

"Stay where you are," called Ted, "I'll come over for a few moments."

Ted asked about Joe and Tom happily told him Joe had done a grand job planting the marrows and they looked fine. They passed a cheery ten minutes and Ted agreed it was definitely time for a wheeler, why not? Definitely time for his pal to 'get mobile' and feeling cheered Tom went home to ring and tell Owen he would give a wheeler a try.

A week later, Tom headed for the church with his new three wheeled walker, he felt pretty pleased with himself, he had managed to walk up to the side gate of the church grounds. It was much easier, not such an effort to keep his balance. He didn't realise how much he had missed his walk to the hill and he checked everything over to see if all was as it should be. He checked the church tower, the Knight's head above the window, he even stopped to look inside the porch covering the doorway; everything was still the same. He was more than satisfied.

As he stood on the hill looking down contentedly, he noticed there was not a soul or a single car in sight and it struck him the scene below had probably not changed at all over the centuries except the lane was no longer a dirt track.

He wandered past the tower towards the next field, finding it quite easy with his new walking aid and he stood looking over the site where the old Manor was said to have been. No doubt, a wooden structure and it was said it had burnt right down to the ground and had disappeared completely long ago. There was no sign of it these days although many had searched where it was supposed to have stood, Tom often wondered what actually happened to it. Suddenly, the rooks made a commotion as something obviously unsettled them and he stopped daydreaming and looked towards the wood. He couldn't see anything and soon the noisy birds settled down and silence fell around the hill.

He went back to the seat near the porch for a rest just as the young Baronet, followed by his dogs shouted, "Morning Tom," as he strode by in a hurry and Tom was immediately reminded of his father old Sir Edward, always on the hill. Tom watched as Ned headed down the path a tall, well-built man, full of energy.

Tom wondered if he had enough energy himself to actually make it to the far corner of the church grounds at the back where most of the family were buried. He hadn't been around that part of the grounds for some time. His Meg, William and young James were all buried there close to each other and many older members of the family were not far away. A few distant ancestors were buried on the front of the hill and Tom always felt at home in the burial grounds. He found it an inviting place and remembered how in the early morning light or evening sun the old gravestones took on a soft warm colour and he felt quite content about being there when his own time arrived and he would join his Meg and the others. He could not think of a better place he would like to be.

As youngsters, he and William believed fervently one of the graves hid the entrance to a secret passage said to be leading under the church. There was nothing as exciting as the thought of a secret passage but they never found anything. Tom knew about the caving systems in the area and always thought any secret passage could make use of a natural tunnel underground but so far, no one had found an entrance or exit near the church, at least, not that he had heard of.

Following the narrow path, Tom set off towards the back corner of the church ground and managed to walk part of the way but decided to turn back as the pathway became overgrown with long grass blocking his wheeler. He must tell Owen, he could come down and do a bit of mowing and tidying when he had time. Carefully looking where he was going Tom did not notice Kath standing near the graves in the corner by the stone wall; she was standing looking out over the fields with her back to him.

As Tom headed back to the seat, he trundled past the old rainwater trough hewn out of black grit stone quarried not far away. The edge of the trough was covered in green slimy moss and it blended well against the damp stonewall of the church. It was almost hidden from view standing in the corner on the opposite side from Tom's beloved seat. These days it was only used by the women who filled their flower vases from it when seeing to the flowers.

There were many similar troughs in the gardens dotted around the village, all made of the same quarry stone. In the past, villagers relied on rain water and Tom knew Meg used to always use rain water to water her precious tubs of flowers by the back door, Liz continued to do exactly the same. Many gardens were still planted with the old-fashioned mix of vegetables and flowers jumbled together and the rainwater troughs were still in use, a blessing when there was a hosepipe ban in dry conditions.

"Hello, Tom." A voice broke into his thoughts and Kath came over and sat beside him.

"Where've you been hiding, Kath?"

Looking down, she plucked at a bit of cotton thread on her blouse trying to remove it before answering.

"I've just been taking a few flowers for our James."

She tried to hide the fact she was feeling low and quickly bent to tie her shoelace as her eyes filled.

They sat quietly for a while before getting up and walking around the tower to the brow of the hill where they stood looking out over the fields. Tom sadly thought of the day he had been working in the bottom field when they brought him the news. The boy had accidently fallen in the fast flowing river whilst playing with the other village lads along the bank. They had all been warned many times not to go down to the river to play, it was too dangerous. Quickly blanking out his thoughts Tom turned to Kath.

Her composure had returned and she looked at the old man's pale face and saw he looked worn and tired. She whispered.

"I'll be fine, Tom, come on, I'll walk you home."

"Aye," he replied.

Tom was born on June 23, Midsummer's eve and the morning of his ninety-third birthday arrived. Early morning mists hung over the fields and the sun was slow to appear through the haze.

"Could be a warm one?" he murmured to himself as he looked through the open window.

The small birds were already busy feeding and the house martins darted back and fore overhead making their usual chitter, chatter noise. He looked at William's clock and shook his head; in the old days, he would have been out in the fields by now and Meg would have fed the hens and geese before starting her other chores.

Tom used to farm three fields, in the two largest he grew wheat and later turned to oats and barley for animal feed whilst he grew various brassicas in the smaller one but his pride and joy were his milk cows and a small flock of sheep kept in the common pasture along with other flocks belonging to the various farms. Along with the poultry, he and Meg had so much work there was never much time to spare.

He could remember his early days so clearly when he was a young farmhand when draft horses were still used for ploughing the fields long before the men shared the use of the first tractors in the village. He thought about the modern tractors nowadays with their enclosed heated cabs. What they would have given for such luxury in his day especially in the depth of winter. Like many others in the district, Tom managed with an old tractor right up until he retired. Maggie still used it for carting small amounts of hay or manure on the little wooden trailer she attached to it and it struck him life hadn't really changed that much in the village over the years.

Tom had been a strong man in his day but as he got older and frailer, the arthritis set in and he seemed to ache constantly. He remembered many a day he got home from the fields soaked to the skin by the cold, wet weather and Meg would plod back and fore with buckets of hot water to top up the old tin bath for him. She always had it ready in front of the fire in the kitchen so he could soak his poor tired limbs before falling asleep in the old chair.

Tom's feelings for Meg sort of crept up on him over the years; at first he struggled with his childhood thoughts about Nell, but although he would always love Nell as a dear friend, those thoughts had slowly slipped away and he knew it was Meg whom he wanted, she made him a contented man. *Look at me now, our Meg,* he thought, too worn out to do my own digging in the garden and he grunted in disgust.

He knew his birthday would be a long day with the family popping in and out but Ted and Joe promised they were going to join him and Owen for a game of dominoes after tea. He felt a bit out of sorts but decided to spruce himself up for his special day. He carefully brushed his thin hair, put on his red bracers under his best sleeveless pullover and going into the kitchen was greeted with a loud chorus of…'Happy Birthday to you'…from Maggie and Liz and their faces beamed as they looked up at him.

He could see them as girls; they hadn't changed much, just with a little grey hair and plumper. The dogs ran over to him straight away waiting for any titbits and he patted their heads. Jess as usual went straight back to Maggie, he was always her dog but Rosie stayed glued to Tom's side as he fondled her silky ears and Liz brought him his birthday cards to open. Every year they went through the birthday ritual and although he sometimes felt grumpy, he secretly enjoyed a bit of fuss, although he would never say so.

It was a grand morning and after taking a short walk to the pond and back, Tom sat outside the backdoor and felt the warmth of the sun on his face. He just settled down to doze for five minutes when he heard Nell's voice in the distance. As he opened his eyes, he saw her advancing slowly towards him, her daughter Tess hovering behind. She looked impressive with her steel coloured hair neatly pinned at the back wearing her summer skirt reaching to her ankles with big red flowers on it. She leant heavily on her walking stick, he noticed it was her Sunday best with the fancy black and silver handle and his eyes fell on the brightest pair of red sandals he had ever seen. She was quite a sight and he remembered how good looking she was when she was young.

"Happy birthday, Tom," called Nell holding onto Tess as she came slowly towards him; Liz spotted them through the window and came out with one of the garden chairs and they helped the old lady into it. Nell looked fondly at Tom and with a chuckle, said, "You've still not caught me up then." And her blue eyes twinkled and were as sharp and bright as ever.

Tess and Liz went to find Maggie, Tom and Nell sat together in comfortable silence. They had been friends for such a long time ever since her family came to the village when she was six or seven. He couldn't remember much about life before Nell, they had grown up together. She and Tom had always been special friends and they continued to be after all these years.

Nell was William's girl until the time inevitably came when they fell out. Tom was well aware of Nell's hot temper and sharp tongue and he remembered the evening William came home red in the face with anger and for days was unapproachable. He and Nell were never the same after that day and when the war broke out, William was one of the first from the village to join up; Tom often wondered if it was to get away from Nell but Meg shook her head, she was not so sure. Nell ended up marrying Jack who was quite a bit older than her but had always wanted her from the first time he set eyes on her. They were wed before William was wounded and sent home from the war.

Tom looked at Nell and suddenly said, "You never did tell me what really happened with you and our William. You always ignore the question."

"Why should I tell you; we fell out. That's all you need to know." She snapped, her eyes flashing. "And then there was Jack and you know the rest." She sighed. "They're both gone anyway, your William and my Jack so none of it matters now." She gave Tom a look that said mind your own business but her face softened as she added, "Aye, you and I, we're the only two left."

She shut her eyes and Tom knew full well she wasn't going to say the reason she'd fallen out with William. Still feeling curious, he could only try and guess but at that moment Liz and Tessa came outside to call Maggie and Tess looked at her mother. "You're supposed to be cheerful on Tom's birthday, Mum, not depressing him."

"Hey, Tom, do you remember our old back privies no toilet paper only newspaper. My mother used to cut it in squares with her pinking shears and hang it up on string. Remember?"

They were off down memory lane.

"Aye and I remember bath night with the old tin bath in front of the fire: we took it in turns in our house." They laughed and Tess and Liz left them entertaining each other.

"Good job it was only once a week if you were last by the time you got in the water was cold." Nell chimed in. "Talk about cold, in winter our place was freezing."

73

"Aye and we went to bed with our clothes on some nights and getting out was worse, onto the ice-cold lino with no mats and the windows full of frost and that was on the inside."

Nell went on, "Do you remember Midsummer Day, the day after your birthday, Tom? Remember how we all used to go over to Long Field in the evenings for the Midsummer Bonfire; they don't do it anymore. My dad swore a good bonfire killed all the germs. These days the young ones seem to stay indoors all the time with their new-fangled games on the television computers." And she grunted. "They seem to sit there inside for hours fiddling with their gadgets. Why they keep doing it, I do not know; not like us out in the fresh air." She paused. "We had some good times though. Didn't we, Tom?" And she looked at him and laughed. They both went quiet keeping their thoughts to themselves.

Later that afternoon, Kath along with Alex and Mark came to wish him a happy birthday and by the time Ted and Joe turned up for the promised game of dominoes later, Tom was glad of a little peace. Just before the boys went off home, Alex asked him about the stories of the bowmen at the church, he had asked his Grandmother Kath about them earlier and she sent him to Tom.

"You come down one of these Saturday mornings and we can go a-walk up on the hilltop. I'll tell you then and some of the other stories. Okay!"

Pleased with the answer, Alex nodded; he liked listening to Granddad Tom's stories and said he would visit as soon as he could.

The men were eventually left to get on with their game and the wood burner was stoked up a bit to keep the evening chill away. A quietness descended over the room as the men concentrated on their moves and the only disturbance was Liz clearing things away. When Tom eventually got into bed that night, he felt satisfied the day had gone well and thought at least he was still alive, he had actually made it to his ninety-third birthday.

A few days later, Tom and Ted sat up on the seat by the porch when Joe spotted them as he took a short cut through the church grounds and stopped to pass the time of day. They started talking about the marrow plants, how well they were growing when Ted suddenly asked, "Shall we enter them in the annual show then; what do you think?"

He went on enthusiastically, "I've made my mind up to enter mine and some onions I'm growing as well; they're real beauties this year."

"Let's do it then; one last fling," Tom answered. "That's if you're willing, Joe."

"Okay with me, ours are doing pretty well," replied Joe and he gave a smile as he left them to it. After Joe disappeared from sight, Ted confided quietly to Tom. "I think Joe is really on the mend."

"Could be?" Tom replied but thinking about it for a moment, he added, "Although some take a longer time to mend than others."

Ted nodded in agreement and after a while changed the subject.

"Are you going to enter anything else besides the marrows then Tom?" asked Ted as he got up to leave.

"I might," shouted Tom in reply settling himself with Rosie at his feet.

Tom sat thinking about the village show as he watched the yews gently blowing back and fore and thought *I won't enter this time, I've had a good run over the years; it's young Joe's turn I'll just help him along a little if he needs it.*

Putting his feet up after dinner, Tom picked up his well-worn gardening book and pored over it until his eyelids grew heavy and slowly closed and his mind wandered from the garden to William and Nell; no wonder they fell out both were stubborn and liked their own way often clashing but when William was sent home wounded from France and was in a bad way. Nell went straightaway to help him every day but he never really recovered and sadly died shortly after the war ended.

Tom sighed, many times he tried to tell William not to be hasty, to wait a bit before he enlisted but it was no good, when he was fired up, he wanted to go there and then, he didn't want to miss any of it. He had been so full of enthusiasm eagerly waiting for his big adventure to begin. Nobody could have stopped him.

Tom made his decision to stay behind on the farm after he was asked to consider it. Someone had to get on with what had to be done, food was top priority and farming deemed vital war work, so he just got on with the job when asked to stay but he well remembered when the war was over a few in the village made comments that cut him to the bone. There had been moments when doubts began to creep into his mind, did he do the right thing. Should he have enlisted with William?

Even now, Tom felt the muscles in his throat tighten a little as he thought of William wounded, feelings of guilt that he was still alive surfaced. He never mentioned anything to anyone how he felt, especially to Meg. She had always just been thankful he was safe and never questioned his decision to stay farming; she believed in him, in her mind he did what he had to do. Nell was the only one who guessed his feelings, she always knew what Tom was thinking and told him straight away not to be so bloody daft, someone had to be sensible and stay behind to do the work and anyway it would not have helped William one bit if he'd gone off to fight with him. Nell well knew William's love of adventure and excitement led him along his chosen path, a path that no one could change. She should know.

When Liz came in to see if Tom was all right, she found him with his head sunk low on his chest, his gardening book still open on his lap ready to slide onto the floor. She gently took the book off him and put it on the small table before quietly tip toeing out through the doorway, pulling the door shut behind her.

The last few days of June, the temperature soared. The heat hung over the village under hot blue skies and the air was heavy and still, it appeared deserted almost like a ghost town. Everyone stayed inside trying to keep cool and Tom kept his window shut with the curtains drawn to keep the heat out of the room.

Liz had gone to town shopping and Maggie was working outside in the barn. Tom nodded in his chair with Rosie stretched out asleep at his feet. The only sound to be heard beside the buzz of a fly struggling to find its way out of the window was the ticking of William's clock. Tom suddenly opened his eyes and wondered where everyone was. Rosie stirred and got up shaking herself before going to sit by his side, her nose nudged his arm, he stroked her soft velvet head and she looked lovingly up at him.

I suppose I'd better get up and look for them 'old girl'.

Rosie stood up and wagged her tail as if she understood every word and gently padded along behind him as they went outside into the bright sunlight.

"Are you there, Maggie?"

"Won't be long; I'll be there in a minute," she shouted wearily from the barn.

He stood by the gate in the shade of the old holly tree looking down the lane and although the hill beckoned to him, he knew a walk would be too much in the afternoon heat. He was too tired and his legs felt heavy; it was an effort for him to walk at all so he went and sat by the back door to wait for Maggie.

He watched a few of the brown hens as they scratched the earth and clucked under the hedge, some nestling down in the warm dust, a sight he had seen many times over the years. It made him smile as he saw the breeze ruffle their feathers, fluffing them up as a few of them strolled about with the old white cockerel mincing along behind them before he strutted off on his own. The sight of the feathers on the hens' legs reminded him of leather chap, cowboys wore in good old cowboy films. He suddenly missed 'the old days'.

As he sat there, a similar warm afternoon came to mind when he had been sent outside to play as he was getting in his mother's way when she was trying to finish her work He remembered meeting Nell her face all smeared with dust and where her tears had fallen there were two white streaks down her cheeks. She had also been in trouble with her mother over something or other and after some persuasion he decided to join her, they would run away together and everyone would be sorry when they found out the pair of them had gone forever.

They didn't get very far, just down the road carrying some clumsy jam sandwiches made with chunks of bread, quickly stuck together with jam and wrapped in newspaper. They ran up to the church and hid around the back in one of the bushes until they were bored. After eating most of the sticky sandwiches, they carefully wrapped up the remainder and crept out of the bushes. They went into the church porch and Nell dared him to go into the church itself. She said if he did, she would and they carefully opened the heavy door and stepped in.

It was dark inside until their eyes became accustomed to the dimness and they stood there not daring to move. They eventually picked up courage and tiptoed up the centre aisle through the chancel arch and Nell in a whisper challenged Tom to touch the altar rail, holding his breath he went up to it and hesitantly held his hand out and ran his hand over the dark oak rail hoping and praying he would not be struck down or punished in some way by God. He laughed to himself thinking about it and remembered how they both suddenly turned and made a very speedy exit down the aisle and through the door.

Outside, they breathed a sigh of relief and went around to the hilltop to check on the world below. Was anyone looking for them? Did anyone care? Feeling a bit disgruntled, they sat on an old tree stump near the stonewall at the side of the church and finish the remains of the sandwiches which were now stuck to the paper. The jam had soaked into the stale bread but with their bare legs dangling, swinging back and fore they finished them off in minutes.

Nell sneaked her hand into his as they sat there and he remembered how he leant over and daringly kissed her cheek just as they heard familiar voices calling loudly. They jumped nervously off their seat, hoping they were not going to get more than a telling off for running away, down the path they ran as fast as they could to tell them they were safe.

Tom trudged slowly behind his father as Nell turned and smiled at him full of bravado, she tossed her head defiantly as she gave him a wave and her mother with a no-nonsense look tugged her by the other hand and marched her off home. Tom knew by the way his father was sternly striding along not saying a word he was probably in for it when he got home and he hoped it was only going to be straight to bed with no tea even though he was starving. Better than any alternative.

The sun sank a little lower in the sky as Tom sat by the back door thinking of those distant days. His and Nell's friendship had never changed over all the years they had known each other. Their bonds forged in childhood had never really been broken and feeling content, he sat there watching the sunset waiting for Maggie.

*

V

The young, newlywed mistress stood on the hill feeling apprehensive. Her husband was away 'til the morrow. He was an ardent supporter of the King, a royalist like many land owners in the area and feeling fearful she felt a strong desire to go into the church to pray for his safe return Cromwell's forces were said to be somewhere in the area not far away'.

Charles the First ruled England and it was less than twenty years since the death of his father James Stuart, distant cousin to Elizabeth and now there was civil war in the land. As the mistress looked out to the horizon searching for any sign of her husband's early return, she looked down over their strong looking Manor House below and wished fervently he would return home soon, this very evening before it was dark.

Her maidservant who stood nearby had already heard much talk of a gathering of the men from the villages and other hamlets to be held down in the valley that evening and she knew it meant trouble. She wanted her Mistress to hurry back down to the Manor House within the walled garden where it was safe. The Master would be angry indeed if he knew they were up on the hill alone. In vain, she tried to tell her young mistress but the mistress set on her course of action told her maid they were in God's hands and continued to go inside the church as planned.

The maid gave a sigh of relief when the Mistress eventually left the dim interior of the church and they hurried quickly down the hill. It was already late afternoon and when daylight faded, the maid knew the men would start to gather and there could be problems for anyone outside of their dwelling that evening. A gathering of men always meant trouble in her eyes. She felt very nervous and was glad when they were back inside the grounds of the Manor heading for the safety of the solid stonewalls of the house.

The boy hid in the church all night and saw as dawn began to break a faint light through the narrow slit opening in the tower behind him. Slowly, he moved from his hiding place at the back of the church and headed towards the heavy wooden door. Outside, the sharp morning air felt cold as he went around to the front of the tower and stood looking down from the hill at the dark shape of the Manor below and over towards the horizon.

He tried in vain to see through the early morning gloom. Maybe he would see some of the men returning to the village and he shook all over as he remembered the evening before. The men had sent him home for he was too young to join them; this was to be a serious gathering. He stubbornly followed at a distance, creeping along behind them hidden from view. He saw the men from further up the valley joining the group and together they all headed down to the meeting place. The boy did not understand the reason for the meeting but his father and older brother were with them, so he followed.

Over the rise they went, through the grassland down towards the long diagonal path that farm animals took, leading to the lower valley. He suddenly heard a noise a bit like distant thunder and stopped to listen. He recognised the sound of hoof beats. It grew louder and louder and frightened he started to run. His heart pounded as he ran faster and faster until he stumbled and rolled down through the nettles, crashing into the bushes. He caught sight of mounted soldiers as they thundered past. He saw flashes of gleaming breastplate armour and round helmets and some carried long swords. He lay there terrified, hurting all over, scratched and stung by nettles. He listened to the noise; there were sharp sounds, cries and shouting from the men. Someone screamed and he shut his eyes tight and put his hands over his ears.

For a long time, he dare not move until it went quiet and in the darkness he crawled out of the bushes on his hands and knees and keeping under cover as much as he could, he headed slowly back up the slope to the village terrified until he saw the outline of the church.

He clambered quickly up the hill to the church and hid too frightened to move, too frightened to go home in case the soldiers were there. He was scared and tried to curl up at the back of the church in the corner of the tower. Occasionally, he tried to keep watch, peering up through the narrow window in the thick stonewall of the tower but he saw nothing but the dark black sky. Going back to the corner, he huddled there shivering with cold. The night dragged on and his eyes drooped as sleep overcame him but he kept waking at the slightest sound.

Although the sun had not yet risen, a pale light appeared across the sky behind the church. As he stood on the hilltop, he realised he must face the coming day. Aching and cold, he limped down the worn pathway under the yews and made his way home back to their cottage but no one was there, the village was strangely quiet. He set off across the common land to the distant fields. Over the slope, he went and in the distance coming up towards him ghostly figures emerged out of the early morning mist. The women helped the wounded who could walk and those who couldn't were being carried by the older men of the village.

The Roundheads had taken many of the men prisoners and left the wounded and the dead for the women and old men to see to. Hot tears of shame and fear rolled down the boy's cheeks as he remembered he had run away and hidden. He stood and watched helplessly, his eyes searching through the early light. He saw more shadowy figures appear and then he saw his mother and older sister weeping as they helped his father to stagger up the slope bleeding from his wounds and he ran down towards them.

His mother's apron and clothing were bloody and torn where she had tried to tear strips of cloth to stop the flow of blood. He was scared, his mind in turmoil. Would the soldiers return and burn the village? His mother looked at him, her face drawn and sad, she said nothing but he knew she wanted him to help. There was no one else for her to turn to. He wondered where his brother was; when would he return?

Thoughts flew through his mind one after the other. How would they all manage until father was better and his brother returned; who would do the work, gather in the crops?

Although young he knew there was much to be done before the bitter winter months ahead and he realised he was the only one left to help. He watched as they continued to struggle up the slope and he stopped crying and wiped his eyes with the back of his hand as he turned to one of the wounded men struggling to get a foothold and took the man's arm. He put it around his own thin bony shoulders so the man could lean on him a little and they moved silently and slowly with all the others up the slope towards the village.

Those who could do so, dropped down near the stream that trickled along at the foot of hill to rest and recover. Some of the men sat hunched over, their heads resting on crossed arms over their knees; too exhausted to move. The dead and dying were slowly taken up near the church under the yew trees where they were administered to in their last hours. The whole village helped where they could and the Mistress arrived with her maid and went from one to the other giving them water praying her husband would hurry back. He would know what to do.

The boy watched as more women appeared looking pale, searching anxiously for their menfolk hoping they were still alive. They tried to show no weakness as they moved around quietly from man to man. The boy watched, his stomach beginning to churn as he stared at the bodies lying side by side beneath the small window in the church tower. He looked away and went over to two clergymen moving amongst the badly wounded lying there under the yew trees. The men who could, watched him approaching whilst others just stared out of eyes misted over.

He swallowed hard once again feeling sick at the sight of the blood and unable to watch anymore, he quickly ran to the front of the tower where he stood trying to overcome his feelings. He suddenly heard his name. He saw his sister near the spring waving and calling to him to come down, his father was asking for him and mother needed him.

The boy turned, once more compelled to look at the bodies of the men with their gaping wounds laid out in a neat row at the foot of the tower. Above the narrow window, the carved head of the knight stared over the dead towards the yews where the wounded sat propped up against the tree trunks the solemn stone face unflinching. The village women quietly tended to the men as best they could, slowly going from one to the other knowing some were beyond help and he turned and ran down to his sister waiting below ready to go home.

*

July was hot and humid and thunderstorms were forecast for the near future. One hot afternoon as Tom made his way to the kitchen looking for Maggie or Liz, he heard the familiar voice of Kath as she appeared in the doorway.

"Hello, Tom, Owen wants to know are you coming up for an hour, he's sitting out in the garden with a cold beer. I've got the car in the lane if you want to come."

She led the way and Tom was happy to have a bit of company perked up as she drove him up to be with Owen.

He lowered himself gingerly down next to his son on one of the garden seats near the kitchen door; it felt nice and cool sitting there in the shade and Tom noticed the splashes of colour everywhere spotting some nice dark green rhubarb leaves hidden amongst the flowers. "The garden's looking good, Owen."

Tom leant forward on his stick noticing all the old cottage garden favourites geraniums, snapdragons and phlox all jumbled together along with the odd vegetable, set off by a number of sweet smelling old pink and white roses. He looked at the mint, chives and thyme growing in all the nooks and crannies, spreading everywhere even between the paving stones. In the distance, he spotted one of his favourites, a bright blue morning glory beginning to blossom over the dry stonewall that stood between the garden and the lane, there was surely no finer colour to be seen anywhere in England. He nodded contentedly.

The bees were busy, noisily working all the flowers and they made the perfect summer sound; the men sat there mesmerised by the sound until Owen suddenly gave a reply to his father's last remark.

"Aye, it does look good. You know its Kath's work out here. She makes a real good job of it. I only see to my veg plot around the back."

"Aye, she always did." And Tom could suddenly see her and Meg with his granddaughters when they were young kneeling side by side in the garden weeding between the shrubs one sunny afternoon, laughing and chatting as they worked. He saw Meg turn to look at him and wave and for a moment, he felt the pain of loss sweep over him knowing she was no longer around. Cheering himself up, he looked at Owen who sat there looking relaxed, a bit of sun worked wonders, Owen was looking well and Tom was pleased.

"Where's Alex then?" asked Tom. "I thought the boys were coming to see me."

"I'll send them down Saturday morning." Owen shut his eyes enjoying the warmth. "Don't forget we're off on holiday soon, renting a caravan like last year; the boys are coming and there's room for you as well if you want to come." He knew very well what the answer would be.

Tom shook his head. "No thanks, I'd be a pest; I'd want to come home as soon as I got there. Anyway, I have to keep an eye on Joe with our marrows. You will be back for the village show then Owen?" Tom looked a little anxious.

"Aye, reckon," Owen replied with a laugh. "I wouldn't miss our show, would I?"

The sound of television drifted through as Kath opened the back door and stepped outside with a tray: "You can stay for your tea if you like Tom, I'll let Maggie know."

Smiling at her, he nodded his acceptance.

"I'll go and make a start then." And off she bustled back inside full of womanly purpose.

As Owen drove Tom back home, they noticed Joe up on the hill standing in front of the church tower and both raised their hands to wave but Joe just stood there as still as a statue. Tom wondered if he was all right or just miles away, lost in thought.

The weather broke a day or two later, dark angry clouds welled up over the fields looking full of menace. Tom stood by his window and watched as the sky turned a strange colour; the birds were quiet, they had disappeared under hedges and the eaves of the barn as the wind picked up. The rain started to fall, slowly at first then faster and faster causing brown muddy soil to spatter up everywhere. Tom was just about to go and sit down when he saw a figure dash by, he realised it was Joe and he got up and tapped the window to catch his attention, signalling for him to come inside. Tom tried to hurry into the kitchen to open the door. "Come in man, come in," he shouted. "What on earth are you doing?"

Joe was soaking wet even with his old, long garden raincoat on and he stood there dripping on the floor, the water running in little river-lets off his clothes. His thick hair hung in matted locks.

"I thought I could get our marrows covered up but I was too late. I'll check them when it stops."

"Come into the kitchen." Tom led the way. "Hang your coat on the back of that chair by the woodstove, I'll stoke it up and put a few more logs in and you may dry out a bit. Sit down and get a warm, Maggie and Liz have just gone to town but they left me a brew so we're lucky." They sat at the table and Tom looked at Joe kindly and eventually asked, "How's things then?"

Joe looked down into his mug of tea. "Not bad, Tom, I have to try and find things to do sometimes to keep busy." He went quiet. "I realise now how she must have felt on times when I was at work, lonely."

They sat and listened to the logs crackling away in the woodstove.

"Was that one of the reasons then, her being lonely?" Tom asked, he realised Joe wanted to talk.

"Partly, she had plenty of reasons and some I'll probably never understand but…" His voice faltered. "Before we met, she lived with a fella who was just a no good…" Joe hesitated shaking his head. "You don't really want to know

89

what he was like." Joe clenched his fists. "She would seldom talk about him but I know he was violent. Anyway, he eventually left her one night taking anything he could lay his hands on with him." Joe stopped, taking a swig from his mug; he stared out of the window for a few minutes before going on.

"When we got together and moved to this area, she managed to find a job and everything seemed fine for a time until she was made redundant." He sighed. "I was working long hours and too tired after work to realise she was unhappy." Joe shook his head. "She just went quieter and quieter, I must have been blind or bloody stupid not to notice." He covered his eyes with his hand. "If only, Tom, if only…" He could not go on and when he looked up his face looked pale and haggard.

Tom gently put his hand on Joe's shoulder and after a while, said, "Joe, you come over here whenever you want, we can just sit, or have a game of dominoes, or just chat about the garden. Come over whenever you like."

Looking at him, Joe replied gratefully, "Thanks, Tom. I will, I'd like that."

Joe's clothes were beginning to dry out a bit and looking through the window again, he saw the rain had eased off.

"I'd better get off home; this weather is here to stay. I'll go before the rain gets any heavier."

Tom made his way back to his room thinking about Joe's wife; on the odd occasions he had seen her, she always seemed very quiet. He vaguely remembered one day he was sitting on his bench by the church and she was standing beneath the yew trees opposite. Although he couldn't remember her face, he did remember that day she did not move just stood, a rather lonely figure staring at the ground. He wondered what had drawn her attention and looking back, he wished he had spoken to her but wishing was no good as well he knew.

Owen dropped the boys off the following Saturday morning as planned. "Send them back when you want to." Owen said with a laugh as he turned to go.

"Aye, they'll be fine until lunch," Tom replied. "I'll send them back to you then so I can get a bit of peace."

Mark the oldest was happy to run off and help Maggie with the chickens and the work in the barn but Alex wanted to go with Tom for a walk to the hill.

"Are you ready, Granddad Tom?" He was keen to be out and on their way. Tom bent with difficulty to put his shoes on and looked at the boy who was kneeling by Rosie lying asleep on the mat. "Can Rosie come with us?"

"If she wants to follow us, she will, lad." The boy nodded and Tom thought how much he reminded him of Owen when he was that age.

They meandered along down the lane towards the duck pond ready to turn up the path by the side of the village hall. As Tom plodded along with his wheeler behind the boy, he looked at the trees in full land caught a whiff of the wet grass and it brought back vague memories. He nostalgically though how he would have been getting ready to do the harvesting before the weather broke. This was the time when the sound of the harvesters and machinery could be heard around the village.

Alex, full of energy like any six-year-old, ran ahead into the church grounds and straight away ran over to the water trough. He immediately tried to stick his fingers into the water through the wire mesh that covered the trough to stop small animals and debris falling into it. He could smell the dank water as he leant over to have a look and fingered the patches of green slimy algae on the sides of the trough pulling a face as he wiped his hands on his trousers.

"The trough's not really full yet," he shouted.

"There'll be plenty more rain to fill it up," Tom shouted back as Alex ran into the porch to wait for him. Tom caught him up and noticed a couple of the house martins flying in and out twittering overhead warning them to keep away but young Alex's mind was on the story.

"Right, now run your hands down the pillars," said Tom and the boy did as he was told. "Can you feel the dents and grooves?" Tom started to tell him the story of the wars with France, how the men had to practise with the longbow sharpening their arrows on the pillars and the chosen men were sent to fight. Alex stood and listened to his great grandfather with his mouth slightly open and suddenly asked.

"Where did they stand to practise then?"

Tom pointed vaguely over towards the yews. "Somewhere between the door and the yews, it would have to be near the doorway wouldn't it, if they sharpened their arrows on the pillars. Remember there was no porch back in those days."

After thinking, Alex nodded and asked, "Did any come home afterwards?"

"I don't know, maybe some did," replied Tom.

Alex nodded again and then looked up at the stone above the door with the carved figures on. "Who are they, Granddad, what are they doing?"

"Well lad, I don't really know, that stone was carved long before the church was built so it is very old."

Alex stood looking at it. "They look like drawings of stickmen running over the ground and that one's fallen in a hole," he whispered pointing to a half figure.

Aye, maybe so, Tom answered thinking to himself or he's chopped in half.

"What else shall we look at?" Alex was ready to move on.

"Let's go to the hilltop and I'll tell you the story of the battle fought near here in the Civil War and we can look at the carved head of the knight on the way."

"How do you know he's a knight?" Alex stood looking up at the carved head.

Tom suddenly began to feel tired with all the questions but answered, "Well, I'm not sure; maybe the owner of all this land had his own head carved on it when the church was first built on top of the hill."

Alex looked at Tom. "I've a really good poster of a knight in full armour." And he added, "I bet he was a Knight." And after a few more questions asked, "I wonder if he was brave?"

"Aye," said Tom, "he probably was."

They wandered around to the front of the tower with Alex still chattering away, He kept asking questions and Tom just nodded in reply.

Tom felt the slight breeze blowing around the hill and he pointed over to the distance and started telling the story of the battle said to have taken place in the area.

"Have you been told in school about the war between the men supporting the King called Cavaliers or Royalists and

93

the men who supported Oliver Cromwell called the Roundheads?"

"Why were they called Roundheads?"

"Because of the plain round helmets they wore." Tom went on, "In this village, all the men supported the King. One day, some decided to gather together with others from the villages around here. They were all going to have a gathering."

Alex looked at Tom. "Like football supporters?"

"Aye." Tom laughed and went on although he was beginning to flag a little.

"The Roundhead soldiers with their Commander were in the area, they heard about the gathering and their Commander sent the horse soldiers called Dragoons to break the gathering up and that's when there was a battle between them."

"What sort of battle?" Alex asked.

"What they call a skirmish. In those days, soldiers used swords and a few had old-fashioned muskets. Anyway, the village men were taken by surprise, many were wounded, some were killed and the rest were taken prisoner."

"Where did it happen then? Was it over there?" And Alex pointed towards the distant fields adding, "How do you know there was a battle?"

"They say it was all written down by the church rector from the next village in the valley and he wrote it all in the records. When we were young like you, we were told all these stories and everyone said the men must have fled downhill being chased, we used to go and look for any signs of a battle down over the fields, hoping to find musket balls or handles of swords but we never found anything."

Although young, Alex was full of enthusiasm for the stories, he suddenly tugged at Tom's sleeve.

"Shall we go back to the farm to see what Mark's doing?"

Feeling a bit thankful, Tom replied, "Aye, I'm getting cold." And they set off towards the side gate. Alex stopped to look once more at the carved head of the Knight and asked Tom again why he was there above the window.

He had stared intently at it and Tom told him maybe the Knight just wanted everyone to know he was once here and the boy thought about it for a moment before answering. "Or maybe he just didn't want to leave Granddad Tom."

"You're right, lad; maybe he just didn't want to leave the hill."

It was time for the garden fete always held in July in the lovely gardens around the manor to raise funds for the church, eagerly looked forward to by the village. Over the last few years, Tom only attended the event for an hour to please Maggie and Liz but decided this year he would stay home. The wet weather of late had played havoc with his arthritis and Nell sent a message to say she wasn't too keen on any garden party either finding them too crowded and full of families with noisy children she would like to join him and keep him company.

Tom remembered when Meg used to always volunteer to give a hand along with Nell, they loved it, the stalls, the brass band, baking cakes for the tea tent, the dressing up for the occasion and Tom went along on occasions when he had the time. Now it was Liz, Maggie and Kath who spent the morning getting everything ready for their afternoon's activities. He wondered if the youngsters of the village were still the same as they were, eager to spend their money on the stalls. He remembered someone else's books or toys always seemed much more exciting than your own.

He decided he and Nell could just sit and snooze near the fire when she arrived; like many older villagers he liked a fire summer or winter, it made the room seem alive and kept the room aired.

Maggie poked her head around the door. "You're definitely not coming then, Tom?"

"No, I'm staying in the warm, looking after my knees." He gave her a cheeky smile and added, "Anyway you know Nell's coming down to nag me."

He settled in his chair and just as his head started to nod there was a knock at his door and Nell appeared with Tess following behind.

"Afternoon, Tom, I hear you want some company."

"Aye, sit down, our Nell." Tom waved to the spare chair and Tess helped her mother into it before leaving. Nell had lived with Tess and John for some years ever since she and Jack's farm became too much for her. These days she was happy living with her daughter as long as she had her own rooms. Nell had two grown up grandchildren, the eldest Kerry was married with children of her own and Glyn still a bachelor was a farmer like his grandfather Jack.

After Jack died, Nell had kept the farm going with hired help but eventually she let Glyn take it over as he was so keen. He was a handsome fellow and Nell and Tom had lived in hopes of him and Owen's youngest daughter Jen making a go of it but they seemed to drift apart when Jen moved with her nursing job down south. It had been a big disappointment to Tom and Nell but they said nothing.

They sat there together with their eyes shut listening to the ticking of William's clock. Tom's room still had the vague warm smell of baking that had drifted in from the kitchen and soon the pair of them started to nod comfortably until Tom suddenly opened his eyes. "Nell!" He grumbled looking at her sitting there. "You're snoring."

"No, I'm not." She snapped.

Still a fiery piece thought Tom and immediately Nell and William came into his mind.

"Why didn't you two stay together, Nell?" He forgot he had asked her the same question a few weeks ago.

"Let it go, Tom." She opened her eyes wide and looked at him with exasperation. "Why do you want to know after all these years? You were on about it the other day, remember."

"It's just William's been on my mind a lot lately," he mumbled but daren't say he was just plain curious.

"Well if you must know" – her eyes narrowed – "we fought over getting married." She gave a snort. "I just didn't want to marry him or anyone at that time."

"Why couldn't you just tell me then?" Tom interrupted.

She lowered her eyes and then looked up mischievously at him her blue eyes as bright as ever. "At one time, Tom I used to think…maybe you and I might…only you went off and got married to Meg." She gave a chuckle.

"Steady 'our Nell', don't start that. I can't cope." He knew she was teasing, at least he thought she was but you never really knew with Nell.

She laughed and then sighed. "The truth is, Tom, he didn't ask me, I asked him as you and Meg had wed and I felt I was missing out." She went on, "He said no to me

97

straight away, he wasn't ready to get married, he wanted some adventures in his life. I was so angry with him I lost my temper and we had a blazing row, I stormed off and you know we never spoke again until he came home wounded from the war." She went silent, glaring at Tom and then abruptly changed the subject and Tom knew that was that. Soon they were both sitting there with their eyes closed and Tom thought Nell was at least telling some of the truth as William was always seeking adventure, he had been more than excited by stories of battles and being sent off to fight in foreign lands.

The following day, Tom went for his walk earlier than usual as Liz and Maggie were busy, Ted and Mary were on holiday for the week and Joe was at work so there was no one he could really have a chat to. He made his way up the path to the side gate of the church grounds with Rosie plodding along behind him. He continued towards his seat by the porch to sit and get his breath back. It was peaceful enough sitting there but he felt a sudden urge to go inside the church.

Rosie lay down to wait for Tom as he opened the door as wide as he could and struggled to get his wheeler in over the worn step. His eyes took longer than usual to become accustomed to the dim light and he stood by the ancient font with its strange carved figures that reminded him of the large stone set above the door before proceeding slowly up the centre aisle.

He noticed the filtered sunlight as it streamed through the beautiful slim glass window near the pulpit, stretching across the chancel arch lighting up the floor with patches of colour. He went over to have a closer look at the old family memorial on the left hand side of the arch. The memorial still looked ungainly, too big for the corner; it stuck right out and spoilt the shape of the original chancel arch and he tried to get a bit nearer staring at the figures kneeling in prayer.

This was the man who built the hall before the civil war but Tom wondered what sort of man he really was devoutly kneeling there opposite his wife hands together in prayer. He knew there were many secrets held inside the old building and when the sunlight suddenly disappeared and dark shadows crept over the floor, Tom felt it was time to go before the whole weight of history suddenly closed in on him.

He managed to get his wheeler through the doorway where Rosie was waiting and eventually made his way towards the seat by the porch.

Tom was drawn to glance up the Knight's head before his eyes suddenly dropped to the ground beneath the narrow window and for no reason he felt sad. Sitting resting his back which was beginning to ache he looked towards the yew trees softly swaying back and fore in the wind making a swishing sound. The sun was hidden behind the clouds which were constantly changing shape as they moved overhead and Tom shivered. Making an effort to get up he stood slowly trying to steady him-self calling to Rosie and they slowly made their way past the yews to the side gate.

Tom stood by the gate waiting for Kath to come in the car to fetch him. He stared at the trees across the road; it was the time of year when they had the full-blown look of summer and he noticed the house martins darting about. They were busy with their young, teaching them to fly and how to feed themselves on the wing in readiness for the time they all took off and disappeared back to the lands they came from.

When Tom could still manage to get upstairs to his bedroom in the farmhouse a few years ago, he remembered a couple of the little birds built their nest of mud right at the side of the bedroom window. Every morning, he watched the nest with interest, how the adult pair worked to build it bit by bit, layer by layer and then the eggs were laid. When the eggs hatched, the tiny chicks eventually poked their little heads up out of the narrow entrance of the nest and made little peeping noises. Like most parents, the adult birds flew back and fore bringing food for their offspring, each bird wearing itself out with the effort. Maggie had not been happy about the nest, she said the birds made an awful mess on the windowsills, down the wall and on the ground below but Tom enjoyed watching them. What did a little mess matter.

"Morning, Tom," called Kath. He was miles away and did not see her arrive; she walked around the car and opened the door for him. "Can you manage?" She folded up his walker and put in the boot of the car.

"Aye," he replied as he got in; he rarely went out of the village these days but decided to go this morning after a bit of persuasion from Liz and Maggie. The weather was dry and sunny although heavy rain was predicted later that evening. At least, he could buy seeds from the small garden store that sold everything. They were for Joe and he would treat himself to a new large magnifying glass. His eyesight was getting worse, and Kath was going to make an appointment for him to get them tested. Even with his reading glasses on, he had difficulties reading lately. He often wondered why they made the print on various packages so small, it made him so irritable.

Tom was wearing his second best tweed jacket over his usual grey pullover and had made an effort with his hair, neatly brushing it back. In general, he gave little heed to how he looked; he never really thought about such things except on special occasions when Maggie or Liz nagged at him. Liz had often told him his weather beaten face had character but he just thought of himself as plain and ordinary so whatever he wore didn't really matter too much.

"Are you warm enough?" Kath asked. "There's a bit of a breeze blowing." She then noticed his woollen scarf hanging from his pocket and thought he's not leaving anything to chance and smiled to herself.

He nodded as he pulled the door of the car shut asking. "Where's Owen then, is he working this morning?"

Owen worked part time these days at the Hall helping with the gardens. He'd retired from full time work some time ago.

"He said he'd be down this evening to beat you at dominoes," said Kath mischievously.

"I'll be waiting then," Tom answered good-humouredly.

They drove on in silence as the car went slowly along the avenue lined with Lime trees leading to the main road. They passed through the village gateway and crossed over the busy main road. Continuing on a small road leading to the narrow back lanes, Kath headed for the quieter route to town with far less traffic.

Tom had not been down this way for ages and remembered as boys they often trudged up and down these country lanes. It was still a beautiful undulating landscape of large fields with cattle and sheep grazing peacefully either side of tall green hedges. Originally, the lanes were tracks for farm animals and they had not really changed much over the years. Although the lanes allowed traffic both ways, there was only room for one vehicle at a time with laybys at intervals for cars to wait whilst vehicles coming the opposite way passed by.

When the car reached the longest diagonal lane that ran down the slope, he remembered as a boy walking with William and the others down to the narrow river when they were young. They always quickened their pace going down this lane; the hedges towered above them casting eerie dark shadows that whispered and made strange noises. Sunny days or grey days, it did not matter; they all walked briskly whistling loudly. The older lads from the village told dramatic stories of dragoon soldiers and gruesome battles and they listened intently and never lingered on their way down this lane. Even now sitting in the car, Tom felt a little uneasy and wanted to look over his shoulder to check what was behind him.

Tom remembered telling young Alex all the stories and he saw himself about Alex's age making his way over the fields looking for William and the other older boys who had run off to play. He remembered wandering across the big open field that ran downhill, feeling really cross shouting William's name. The wind picked up and whined as it blew over the open grassland and he began to feel scared thinking of the stories of dragoons, soldiers on horseback with swords. He fancied he could hear the horses galloping, it seemed to get louder. He became so frightened he threw himself down on the grass, shutting his eyes, his hands over his ears.

When he eventually scrambled up, he headed home to the village as fast as he could and only when he saw the hill come into view did he feel safe. From then on, he kept away from that area on his own and only went down that way with William or the others but he never told them about his adventure, they would have laughed at him.

The town was very busy that morning; it was market day. The old cobbled square by the White Swan was full of stalls and the main road was equally full of cars all trying to get into the main car park in the town centre. Kath was glad they were there reasonably early; she knew all the free places to park the car in the side streets making it easier to go where they wanted to go without much effort.

These days, Tom felt a bit bewildered by the town with its bustle and noise and he did not really appreciate the modern shops with their gadgets for sale; new-fangled radios and computers and all the paraphernalia that went with them. They never had such things in his days and he did not understand the need of the young to possess them.

After purchasing his magnifying glass, Kath left him to slowly make his way to buy seeds in the small corner store that had not changed over the years. It sold all types of garden tools, nails and screws, household bits and bobs, seeds, plants, twine and even pet food. Tom enjoyed poking about having a look. He liked the smell of the old shop with its sacks of dog biscuits, wood shavings and sawdust for rabbit hutches. It reminded him of long ago. After passing the time of day with the shopkeeper, he was eventually glad to go and sit on one of the seats in the market square just opposite. He sat near the old pub where he could watch everyone coming and going and was content to wait for Kath to return.

In the old days, the cobbled market square was the place to buy all your dairy and garden produce, seeds and farming tools. He remembered the women scurrying about wearing hats carrying woven wicker baskets, not these plastic carrier bags. The café called Nellie's had once been the old bakery where the smell of fresh baked bread wafting from the large oven made your mouth water. Outside the Royal Oak, the men would gather to discuss prices and day-to-day events in the farming world. How different everything seemed these days, shopping done in big super markets and farming had completely changed from his time. Some said things had changed for the better, but Tom really missed the old world, his world, he sometimes had the feeling he somehow did not belong in the new.

All the older generation grumbled the young had too much of everything and Tom agreed it was not good for them, they also thought the young did not know the real meaning of hard physical work but he liked to give them the benefit of the doubt. "We did though, we knew how to work," he muttered to himself. He watched a youth with long hair leaning against the wall listening to some tune or other through the earphones attached to a small radio, tapping his foot in rhythm as he joined in singing all out of tune. Laughing to himself, Tom just shook his head. The young these days were a mystery.

After Kath had finished her shopping, they were soon driving out of the busy town on the main road, heading back home up the steep hill leading out of the town. The view as they went over the top leaving the town behind was the best bit for Tom, the whole countryside stretched out before him. The sight made him feel almost excited to be on his way back to the village. It lifted his spirits.

They reached the old coaching inn and soon the car turned off the main road between the two worn pillars of the old gateway. They headed down towards the village. Tom felt himself relax driving onto familiar territory. This was his world, slower, greener, where the avenue lined with trees seemed to welcome him. Kath always drove slowly as the sheep with their growing lambs and even cattle tended to wander back and fore over the road. The estate remained much the same as it ever was. It still had the demesne land, the meadows, common pasture and woodland besides the large fields rented by the farming tenants and Tom knew every contour of the estate by heart.

"If you let me out here, Kath, I can have a walk back, it will do me good."

"Okay if you're sure. I can drop you further along just before the green where the old horse chestnut trees are, if you like."

"No, here will be fine thank you."

She stopped the car and got his wheeler for him and as he straightened himself up, he took a deep breath of fresh air. As she drove off, he stood a few moments steading himself and took in the scene in front of him. He started to walk to the crossroads feeling the intense pleasure he always felt at the sight of the stone cottages now in view. Even though it was summer, there were wisps of smoke lazily curling up into the sky from some of the chimneys. Seeing the horse chestnut trees standing in the middle of the grassy area they called 'the triangle' made him feel he was meeting old friends and he stopped not only to admire them but to get his breath back and to look up at the hill with the church. Now he was home and he felt happy.

He saw the worn gravestones clustered around the church in their familiar way as over the years they sunk into friendly angles towards each other. The crumbling stonewall with the wooden gate was covered in soft green moss and the large oak trees standing in the next field hung their branches over the wall as if to protect it. Tom's eyes followed the path that wandered up to the yews. There had been yews up there since the Middle Ages and he couldn't ever imagine the church grounds without them. He trundled along the lane to the duck pond. Although his legs ached and he felt tired, he was somehow drawn to go up to the side gate of the church grounds to stand on his hill for a few moments. He breathed in the cool fresh air as he stood on the hill.

It was time to go, Rosie would sense he was nearby and he knew she would be standing by the farm gate eagerly waiting to greet him. As he passed the tower, he began to feel a bit unsteady and stopped to rest a little on his usual seat opposite the yews. He sat there content, he was back where he belonged. There was nowhere else he wanted to be but he wondered why on some occasions there was a feeling of quiet almost sadness around the trees.

*

VI

The hill changed little after the Civil War and village life was relatively quiet through the years until Charles Edward Stuart, son of James Edward Stuart, the 'Old Pretender' was on the march to claim what he considered his right to the English Crown. The rebel army was heading down through England just west of the village on their way towards London. The rumour was there were thousands of men marching with him and they needed more horses.

As the rebels marched nearer, after some deliberate thought the landowners in the area decided to send their prime stock out of sight. They were taking no chances; they would move their finest horses, leaving behind the older, weaker animals.

The Lord of the Manor stood on the hill in front of the tower, a tall figure in the moonlight, looking towards the west. He had made his decision to stand with the others and also move his best mounts, he was not going to help any rebel cause and he would give the order right away. His instructions were to get the horses out of the stables as soon as possible and the head groom hastily repeated the orders. They were to move the young strong thoroughbreds leaving the weaker stock. The horses were being sent away, hidden in outlying farms over to the east of the estate where there was no sign of the rebels.

"Get the horses ready." The head groom yelled as he hastily tried to take charge of the men who rushed to help. Some holding lanterns high followed behind those running to do the head grooms bidding. He shouted at them to go steady but the animals already stressed by the noise were frightened by the men rushing around holding lanterns. They started to rear and plunge and there was panic.

The flickering lights pierced the darkness as the men ran back and fore. The terrified animals thrashed about and it was chaos. In the mayhem, the stable boy, the youngest son of the village blacksmith, slipped and was trampled by the horses, his older brother tried his hardest to help but he slipped on the cobbled stones and also fell under the thundering hooves. Someone dropped one of the lamps and a fire started to spread through the stable block. It was altogether a bad night's work.

Dragging his left leg as he limped through the side-gate of the Manor garden into the enclosed walled vegetable area, the middle-aged worker struggled to carry a large wicker basket under his weak almost lifeless arm. One of the kitchen maids at the Manor had asked him to collect the day's vegetables ready for the cook. He cursed under his breath, it was slow hard work for him to get from one area to another and as usual, he grimaced remembering how strong he was when young before his accident. He shut his eyes and for a moment reliving horse's hooves coming down remembering the fierce pain before he lost consciousness.

As he made his way back to the kitchen, his father came to mind, he could see the large muscles on the old blacksmith bulging as he worked. He could hear the sound of the hammer as it forged the iron and the hiss of the hot metal as it was plunged into the water tank to cool. He still remembered all the familiar tools, some handed down, some his father lovingly fashioned himself, working hard in the heat of the forge to make them. He could still see the ancient bellows that leant against the wall in the corner, taller than he was as a boy. His father always told him when he was strong enough to lift the bellows he would be old enough to be a blacksmith's apprentice.

There had been more than enough work for an apprentice; horse shoes to be made, mending the cartwheels and all the farm implements, even making steel hoops for barrels. The idea of following his father and grandfather as village blacksmith was now over, finished, all gone just like his poor brother buried on the hill. He always knew even when he recovered from that night's disaster he would never again be strong enough to be a blacksmith and when his father died another family from north of the village took over the forge. It was a bitter loss that filled his heart.

The full weight of despondency descended upon him and he hung his head not looking where he was going. He suddenly caught his foot on some roots sticking up in the grass and his body jarred as he went down. Struggling to his feet, he felt his usual surge of anger rising up inside him for he knew it would always be this way and he cursed heavily under his breath. He tried hard not to feel so bitter but it was sometimes more than he could bear.

The master gave instructions to his bailiff to make sure he was given work helping where needed around the estate. In some villages, he knew he would have been left to fend for himself. He was also fortunate to live with his oldest sister and her family in their cramped cottage although he had to help work and pay his way. She was a good woman and her man worked hard on the land with their two sons and somehow they managed to survive and cheering a little, he felt grateful he was not left to starve.

When the working day was done, some of the men gathered outside in good weather to smoke a pipe and share the gossip; they were all eager for any news that came their way. They wanted to hear about the troubles and unrest amongst workers in other villages. They knew it was always the same old problems, high taxes, low wages and bad conditions. In this village, they were treated reasonably well and many of them sat quietly, nodding and listening sucking on their clay pipes.

One late afternoon after work was done the pain in his legs and back made him more irritable than usual; he felt restless and stifled being inside the cottage. He got up and limped outside for some fresh air; he made his way down the lane to the foot of the hill. He had a sudden yearning to go up on the hilltop to feel the cool breeze that always seemed to blow there. It made him feel he was alive.

It had been some time since he attempted to go up the hill to the tower and blanking his mind to his pain, he started the slow climb up the path to the church. It took him a long time but eventually he stood leaning against the corner of the tower to get his breath. He moved to look up at the stone head above the narrow window that faced south and as he remembered, the carved features calmly stared straight ahead.

He made his way slowly around to the front of the tower and stood as best he could on the brow of the hill looking over the graves in front of him and his eyes searched out the narrow mound halfway down the hill near the dry stonewall. He felt an empty loneliness creep over him as he remembered his young brother.

That night, still vivid in his memory appeared, he saw the horse being led by his brother; the animal suddenly reared up and plunging about caused two other horses to panic. His brother slipped and fell rolling over as the horses kicked and thrashed about and he remembered how he rushed in to try and help, but too late. As he tried to drag the boy's poor battered body clear, he looked up and saw the hooves coming down, they felt like hammers and he blacked out with pain.

He couldn't remember much about the fire that burnt down part of the stable but he did remember how long it was before he could even move. After the event, when he recovered enough to get himself around; he took the only thing he possessed and struggling up to the grave, he put it on the pitiful burial mound. It was his precious horseshoe. The shoe was the first he completed as a youngster, the one his father allowed him to keep. His first attempts were not good enough for the old blacksmith but he worked each day until with sweat running down his face in the end he managed to make a reasonable horseshoe and his father pleased told him to keep it to remind him to work harder.

Eventually, he spotted the small narrow mound about halfway down; it was now completely overgrown with long grass and hard to see. Glumly, he turned away knowing he would not be able to struggle down to it and there was nothing he could do as the mound had sunk down with time.

No one talked about that night any more it was rarely spoken of. Charles Edward Stuart himself seemed to be forgotten along with all the stories, including the tale of the rebels who for some reason shot the landlord of the old inn down in the valley. They had heard how the men were all caught and hung from the nearby bridge.

The sun began to dip lower and he saw the hazy smoke drifting up from below and heard familiar sounds, he lifted his head. Staring towards the fields where the farmhands had been working late finishing their tasks, the men were beginning to make their way home some carrying long scythes over their shoulders. Calling to each other, he heard the younger ones shouting and taunting each other, full of banter their voices strong and clear. Eventually, they went their separate ways and once again, he stood surrounded by silence as the sun sank lower down.

He suddenly saw his sister's two boys as they came into view. They were late from the fields having just finished working alongside their father and he called down to them. They were strong lads and still had enough energy left after a long day's work. They saw him and strode up the path each of them jesting with him as they stood on the hill by his side. The sun was now down near the horizon and they tried to encourage him to come home with them, back to the cottage, they were hungry, ready for food but he shook his head, he would stay on the hill awhile longer.

He listened as the wind picked up blowing through the yews and he watched the grass as it moved back and fore, rippling over the many graves that had over time become part of the hillside, nothing seemed to change. Suddenly, he heard the sound of a pheasant calling nearby and caught sight of the bright plumage as it emerged from the grass down by the spring followed by some drab little females almost invisible in the setting sun and he smiled to himself, his spirits lifted and he decided he would make his way to the cottage, somehow his pain had eased.

*

Tom stood at the open scullery door and took a deep breath of fresh air thinking of the month ahead. It was the first day of August known years ago as Lammas Day or Loafmas Day when the first fruits of the harvest were celebrated with the giving of a baked bread or fruit loaf to your loved one. *Soon it'll be the end of summer*, he thought. We would have made a start on harvesting already in this good weather. He remembered in days gone by he used to watch the older men with their scythes open a passageway for the binding machines to enter the fields. All the workers were taught to use the scythe and after a long day's work, your whole body ached like hell.

The sun was at its highest and Tom wandered over to sit in the shade of the old tree that stood at the corner of the yard opposite the barn. It always produced lovely cooking apples and still provided Liz with plenty of fruit to bottle and to put in the freezer and there were always apples left over to give away to anyone who wanted them.

It was one of Meg's favourite trees and he would on occasions go and sit on the old bench underneath it where she sometimes sat doing her mending. She loved to sit there in the shade of the cool leaves and used to say they always looked much greener looking through them to a blue summer sky. She always said there was not a better sight in spring when it was fleetingly covered in blossom.

The week went by quickly and he sat with his window open to catch a bit of cool air, suddenly he heard the sound of a tractor in the distance and wistfully wished he was out there working with the men like he used to be when he was young; he could almost smell the ripe fields of grain. August was a great month especially when the weather was good and there was always an excitement approaching harvest time. He loved it.

When he and William were young, just like their grandfather before them their father worked on the large spread out farm a mile away near what used to be the old railway line. As boys every year, they helped with the hay making and Tom suddenly thought of all the old fashioned tools the farming men used. He could see them all clearly, the different rakes for the hay and even something called a spud to remove thistles and a mattock to dig potatoes. The men use these tools at various times and he could see them all lying in the shared hay wagon ready to be taken out into the fields. He chuckled, there was nothing like riding the hay wagon listening to the rumble of the wooden wheels as they lurched along down the lane behind the huge gentle carthorse.

He looked out of the window at a vapour trail from a plane moving slowly across the sky. *It's getting pretty warm,* he thought just as Joe came into view.

"Nice day, Tom," he called.

"Aye, hope it stays like this for the show. Your marrows should do pretty well, Joe, they look good."

"You mean 'ours'."

"No, they're yours; you've done the work. Maggie and I have decided to show a few summer cabbages instead."

Joe gave Tom one of his rare smiles. "I'm hoping they do really well, Tom." And he hurried off to check everything.

When Kath and Owen returned home from their holiday on the Friday, Tom couldn't wait to telephone Owen about the show the following weekend. After asking quickly did they have a good time, he went straight into the problem, how to get the prize cabbages to the village hall.

"Okay, I'll be there to carry for you," Owen answered with a laugh knowing Maggie and Liz would have done it but he knew Tom wanted him there. He asked how many they were showing and then he asked if Joe was seeing to the marrows. Tom put the phone down feeling satisfied everything was in hand. It was going to be a big day.

When Maggie carefully planted the cabbages Tom had given her instructions, he remembered telling her on many occasions the exact spacing between each plant determined the size of the cabbage heads. She listened to him without grumbling and did all he asked bowing to his years of experience. This really pleased him and indeed each full-grown cabbage looked magnificent. Tom had always in the past grown herbs in between his brassica plants to keep pests away, there was nothing like thyme, sage and mint in between and he swore by planting them in soil that had grown peas the season before, he knew it helped.

These days, he was content to just sit and direct Maggie and felt pleased with the result. Joe's marrows looked real beauties; he was showing six all polished to perfection. Ted had entered his favourite prize gladioli beside his selection of onions and marrows. This was just like the old days and Tom almost felt young again. In fact, he felt as if he had a spring in his step.

Saturday arrived and the village hall was a hive of activity, the tables were set up and produce carefully arranged, the exhibitors came from all the small villages and hamlets in the surrounding area, full of expectations. Outside, picnic tables and chairs for refreshments were set up and the women were in their element sorting out scones, cakes and sandwiches in the kitchen. The exhibitors were adding their last touches to flowers, fruit and vegetables which all looked in peak condition, each apple was shining red or green depending on the variety, carrots were all the same length lying side by side and Joe's marrows looked perfect. They were all pleased at the turnout and everyone said it was the best-looking show ever, although every year they said the same thing.

The judges slowly walked around the tables with their clipboards whispering and nodding to each other and the atmosphere became a little tense amongst the competitors. Tom looked at Ted and thought, *Yes, he is taking it very seriously in fact he was looking a bit pale*. Mary stood by Ted and Tom noticed she took his hand for a few moments. Nell sat watching the proceedings happily chatting to her son in law John as she blew Tom a kiss. The results would be announced after the refreshments and some of them trooped noisily outside while the judges retired to make their final decisions.

Everyone excitedly waited for the judges to come to their decisions and announce the results and as expected Joe took a gold for his marrows, everyone cheered as he collected his certificate. Tom and Maggie's cabbages won a silver/gilt certificate and young Robin from over hill took the gold and Tom smiled and nodded at him shouting, "Bravo, lad."

Tom whispered to Maggie as she sat there, "I would have been quite happy with a bronze."

She laughed.

"Anyway, it must have been your planting, Maggie, you've inherited green fingers from somewhere." And she laughed again feeling in high spirits.

Ted won a silver/gilt for his marrows but his gladioli were second to none – top prize, gold and to Ted's sheer delight, he won 'Best in Show'; they were truly magnificent.

Tom looked over to Owen who was happily discussing the merits of organic growth with a few of the other men when Nell's grandson, Glyn, came over to see how he was and Tom pleased to see him held his hand out.

"How are you doing, lad? I haven't seen you for a long while."

"Can't grumble, Tom, but you know how it is on a farm; hard going on times."

Tom nodded. "Aye, keeps you at it."

The afternoon was altogether a great success and the money raised went to the village's chosen charity for that year. Over the centuries, the village donated money to many good causes; the fact was even recorded in the church records. Everyone was in a good mood having enjoyed the day; it had all been worth the effort.

That night, Tom lay in bed thinking what a good day it had been although Ted had left early not feeling too well. *He must have been over working and picked up a bug,* thought Tom and he promised himself he would go over and see him in the morning, first thing.

The church bell slowly rang out; each chime ending before the next one began. Solemnly, Ted's sons and four grandsons carried the coffin silently on their strong shoulders from the cottage. They headed past the village pond turning to the right to go through the main church gates. They slowly proceeded up the steep drive to the porch entrance. The procession behind the coffin was followed by the rest of the family. They were followed respectfully by Ted's closest friends and many of the villagers. Mary helped by her daughter was waiting by the porch.

Tom and Owen walked along behind the family and Tom felt his son's hand gently on his shoulder, he had insisted on being part of the procession, even for a short distance as soon as he knew they were going to carry the coffin from the cottage like in the old days. The group moved slowly along and Owen steered Tom with his wheeler up to the side gate of the church knowing it would be easier for him. They stood opposite the porch and waited for the main procession to arrive up the steeper slope of the church drive.

Tom listened to the mournful sound of the bell and as the young bearers with the coffin stood waiting to proceed into the church, he noticed some of Ted's beloved gladioli lying in full glory on top of the coffin. His throat tightened as he thought of his poor friend and he looked at Mary her head bowed holding tightly onto her daughter's arm going to take her place inside the church. As he and Owen slowly followed the others, Tom remembered his Meg; it was springtime and he saw the pale yellow of primroses placed on her grave. They were always her favourites and biting his lip hard he went to sit down with Owen and Kath, next to Maggie and Liz.

The service ended and Ted was laid to rest and before making their way to the village hall Tom and Owen stood outside not far from Nell who was sitting quietly in her wheelchair with Tess standing at her side. Tom looked at Nell but made his way alone to the brow of the hill. Owen patiently waited for him leaving him to have time to say goodbye to his friend in his own way.

Tom looked sadly down over the familiar scene below leaning heavily on his wheeler. He and Ted had many a laugh or an argument together as they stood up on the hill nattering and he wondered what life would be like now Ted had gone. He sighed and felt the sense of loneliness creep over him as he stood there watching the grass ripple across the hillside. It's just the way it is he thought as he turned with a heavy heart and saw Nell by his side, they had many times stood together to say goodbye to someone. Nell put her hand up and touched Tom's arm and he held it tightly against his arm. After a while, she left him as Tess took her to see Mary and the others in the village hall.

Inside the village hall, Tom stared around the room; it had all happened so quickly he couldn't believe it was only a couple of weeks ago they were in the same hall for the garden show enjoying themselves. The low murmur of

119

voices could be heard above a piece of soft music and Tom kept thinking how Ted loved a laugh, and a good time, he wouldn't really want them to be so quiet and sad.

"When it's my turn, Owen," whispered Tom, "make sure we have a brass band and lots of cheery stuff, okay?"

"Aye," Owen answered smiling to himself.

Ted's oldest son suddenly called them all to order and in a quiet voice he spoke lovingly of his father and mentioned how happy and proud Ted had been with his 'Best in Show' award and eventually he ended by asking them all to raise their glasses to Ted. Tom's eyes fixed on Mary as her hand shook and she bravely tried to stop the tears.

After Ted's funeral, Joe continued to work and help Tom with the garden; he sat outside with him one afternoon by the back door having five minutes from planting out a few late 'January Kings'.

"I'll start to clear up soon, turn the soil over when I can. That's if you want me to, Tom."

Tom just nodded feeling down. Nothing seemed to make him feel cheerful not even the thought of doing some planting; Joe reading Tom's mind murmured.

"Ted would like to see us plant a few winter cabbages Tom; you know what he was like."

"Aye, you're probably right," Tom answered shakily and went on. "I knew him over sixty years, Joe, and I'll really miss him. He was always working in his garden, full of energy, getting into hot water with Mary. I can't believe he's gone." He looked at Joe and sighed. "Am I getting on your nerves?"

"No, you and Ted did me a power of good and I'm going to miss him myself but if we get on with things…" He trailed off before adding, "As if he was still here. It would sort of help, wouldn't it?"

"Aye." Tom perked up a bit; he decided to go and get the catalogues out that Maggie had brought him from town. He thought maybe he and Joe could continue to work together as Owen was short of time these days between one thing and another. Joe certainly seemed to enjoy coming over the farm to work in the garden and Tom knew he liked a bit of company; much as he did himself and it kept them both busy.

August came to an end and the whole village got together for the annual barbecue knees-up. In the old days, the gathering happened after the harvest was brought in, now it was traditionally on the first Saturday evening in September. The old flat lorry once used for transporting hay bales was brought in for the local country and western band to use as a stage. The village was closed to public vehicles and only the villagers and their extended families were invited to the festivities. It had been the estate's way of saying thank you and the present owner continued the old tradition, joining in the festivities.

It was usually held on the triangle of grass under the large chestnut trees in front of the hill. As dusk approached, the villagers started to walk down the lane from the cottages past the manor joining those from the back lane who walked past Tom's farm and the pond. Everyone seemed to be carrying something, folded canvas chairs, plastic tubs of food; bottles of wine and fruit drinks for the youngsters. The older children carefully carried lanterns made of jam-jars with small candles inside and as the daylight faded away, they looked like a procession of fire-flies bobbing along the lanes.

Blankets were carried to tuck around the knees of older members of the family, to keep out the cold. Large trestle tables had been set up laden with boxes full of bread rolls, buns and cakes. There were tubs of applesauce, pickle, ketchup, paper plates, take away cups for tea or coffee, all laid out ready. A whole roasting pig was turning on a spit and the smell wafting through the air was wonderful. When the word was given, everyone queued up for slices of pork in round buns with baked potatoes and beans or alternatively there were hot dogs and onions and the satisfied villagers staggered off with their hands full.

The night got into full swing when the music started up. The younger children were so excited, jumping around, allowed to stay up late. There was lots of play wrestling dancing and just plain chaos and noise. The older lads hung around pretending to be bored; they casually exercised themselves by pushing and shoving each other about whilst keeping an eye on the girls who pretended to ignore them, looking a million dollars. Tom laughed and thought not much has changed over the years; the young are still the same.

Nearby, Nell in her wheelchair sat with her tribe and Tom waved although she could hardly be seen wrapped in her hat and scarf to keep out the chill night air with a rug over her knees. Even Mary was nearby with her daughter's family, she was making a big effort as she knew Ted would want her to be there, he never missed the annual knees-up, he loved it.

Tom beckoned to Nell to come over but typical Nell she shook her head and shouted for him to come over next to her. He laughed as he was reminded of when they were young she was always so contrary. He drifted off into the past; remembering in their day you had to grow up quickly, when you left school you had to go to work, there was no alternative but at least living in the village with the church and the hill, you had fairs and festivities to brighten up the year.

"Hello, Tom, having a good time?" Joe came over to see how he was.

"I'm all right, Joe. Where're you sitting?"

Owen offered him a beer. "There's plenty of chairs, sit down for a while, Joe, the others are dancing or being daft somewhere."

He pointed to a seat next to Liz who was resting her feet for five minutes and Joe sat down; soon the two of them started chatting about their old school days. Joe discovered although he was a good few years younger than Liz, they went to the same school down in the town before his family left the area and they both remembered some of the old teachers. Joe and Liz nattered away like old friends and Tom looked up to the tower on the hill; he could just pick out a few flickering lights up there in the darkness. For a moment, he wondered what the small lights were until he realised a few of the older lads were racing about carrying jam-jars with the remains of the small-lighted candles inside.

He wistfully thought oh to be young again, they were so full of life showing off to each other, the boys taunting and teasing the girls and as the music played on, they were all in such high spirits. Tom suddenly missed poor old Ted; they would have been chatting about what to plant next season, probably having a few arguments over this or that and in general having a good time. Owen looked at Tom and told him to put away his long face. "Ted wouldn't want to see you looking miserable."

The band was having a break and Liz suggested they have a sing-song like they used to. Owen and Liz started to sing the old medley of tunes including some of Ted's favourites. Tom went over to sit by Nell managing to get his wheeler over the grass and Tess moved for him to sit down next to her. Slowly, everyone started to join in singing until their voices rose in harmony and the night finished in grand style with all the old songs echoing around the hill.

At last, some decided to call it a night and headed off home. Joe made his way up the hill and stood looking down as one by one, the families picked up their belongings to leave. Halfway up not far from the stonewall, he tripped over something solid and bent down to loosen it eventually pulling it out of the ground. It looked like an old rusty horseshoe and he wondered where it came from. He was going to throw it over the wall into the next field but stopped and for some reason just gently put it down amongst the soft grass.

Tom looked for Joe to say goodnight and spotted him in the moonlight, standing on the hill. He wanted to go and join him, the spirit was willing but he knew he was too tired and weary he didn't have enough energy to struggle home; Owen had to rescue him and help him back to the Farm.

As Tom stood alone by his back door after Owen had returned to the others, he looked up and saw the bright night sky and he remembered a similar warm summer's night.

When he and William were young before they left school to go to work, they begged to be allowed to sleep out in the old barn along with some of the village lads. It was after some do or other, he couldn't remember exactly what. To begin with, they had a definite no from their father but eventually he relented after a lot of assuring him of their good intentions and they rushed off to tell the others the good news. He remembered his mother had been more than doubtful but she too agreed after much promising to get on quietly with their chores with no grumbling the next day. When Nell heard about the adventure she was put out, not being allowed the same privilege, she was so cross she refused to speak to any of them for a week.

When everyone had settled down and gone to bed and the noise ceased, stillness descended over the village but the lads still full of energy and excitement couldn't sleep so decided to liven up the night. They began daring each other. It ended with them zipping around after midnight without a stitch of clothing on, laughing and larking around until the early hours.

The next morning, their parents found out as old Mrs Johnson had got up in the night for a drink of water, looked out of her kitchen window to be frightened to death by their antics. They were all punished and the older ones got a thrashing for frightening the terrified old lady. He chuckled to himself, what a night it had been, what freedom they felt and the stars, he had never seen the night sky look so splendid. They ran and cavorted around the village, racing up the hill to touch the church tower and back down, just like wild colts. He laughed to himself remembering that night so clearly, it was magic, the best night ever.

Tom gazed at the sky everything looked and smelt exactly as he remembered; time may have slipped by but the hill, the church, the tower seemed to always be there always the same, maybe they never altered and suddenly feeling more cheerful than he had of late, he opened the back door and stepped into the brightly lit scullery.

*

VII

As the early morning sun began to glimmer through the mist, a figure stood on the hill listening to the rooks. Their raucous noise slightly irritated him but when they settled down and a silence descended, he heard the distinct sound of a robin nearby. The little bird was perched on a gravestone watching him with its sharp beady eye, head cocked on one side. Autumn was not far away and in the morning light, the small bird was a cheerful sight with his red breast.

The Baronet's thoughts were elsewhere. He'd recently returned from a trip to London which always had a bad effect on him. He did not feel comfortable seeing the huge amount of wealth contrasting with so much grotesque poverty in the many areas of the great city. His thoughts flitted to the Prince Regent, everyone knew the gossip how he spent vast sums of money on clothes and fripperies and seemed to live purely for pleasure; his debts were beyond belief as he happily indulged himself to the full. He was already beginning to pay the price; his father George the Third was near the end and it was said the prince would not see many years as king.

The Baronet knew all the court gossip through his sister who married well and lived in London during the season.

She had an ear for such things and years ago, the prince had dallied with a close friend of hers, or so the tittle-tattle story went. She was there when Arthur Wellesley, returned to England a hero after the defeat of Bonaparte; he was welcomed by the Prince who stood in for his father due to the King's increasing spells of mental illness and even then everyone said the Prince Regent did not seem to take his duties seriously.

The Baronet sighed as he looked across to the horizon and was more than happy to be home in the quiet serenity of his estate. Having inherited the land some years earlier with all it entailed, he accepted his fate with mixed feelings. His father had died unexpectedly and now all this was his. Being of a serious nature his profession by choice would have been the church but as the eldest son it was not to be and he keenly felt the responsibilities that now lay upon him.

He noticed the motionless sheep grazing in the fields below, they were by instinct eating as much as possible on the new autumn growth, getting ready for the colder months ahead. He loved to stand on the hill looking out over the land below and his eyes wandered from the sheep to the wood where the old yew stood with its heavy branches and huge trunk, so old no one knew for sure how old it really was.

He suddenly remembered he was on the hilltop to look for a reasonable spot to plant his newly acquired horse chestnut trees but his thoughts had slipped to more important issues. Over the years, he had watched the everyday struggle for survival by the villagers witnessing the working man's life of hardship with few pleasures and he was determined to try and improve and help in some way.

He made his way around the tower and watched the yews opposite the church door, their branches swaying back and fore in the breeze and he stood looking at the church door. Standing in front of the magnificent Norman doorway, he suddenly decided it would be a good idea to have it protected from the weather by a porch. Making his mind up to go inside the church, he stood a few moments longer drawn to look at the carved stone head of the knight above the window, he always expected the expression to alter in some way but it never did.

He nodded to himself as he stepped into the ancient building, his eyes falling straight onto the font situated nearby in the centre aisle with its strange carvings of birds and animals. Although he knew the carvings represented creatures and stories from the ancient Bestiary Book, somehow it always made him feel unsettled. He slowly continued up the aisle towards the family monument at the side of the chancel arch. He went over to have a better look at the figures, admiring the carved rather austere figure of his distant ancestor kneeling in prayer, the one who not only built the present manor but added the beautiful oak rail in front of the altar.

The carved monument looked so cramped in the corner of the church, spoiling the shape of the chancel arch. He stood back and looked around the small church; it needed more space. The wooden gallery at the back made it gloomy and dark although it was unused these days, deemed no longer safe. He realised the church would look bigger without it and there would also be extra light. Yes, he made up his mind, the work would be done.

Suddenly remembering the chestnut trees which had totally disappeared from his thoughts, he retraced his steps to the brow of the hill and decided a good place to plant them was on the land in front of the hill. He knew it would please his wife to see the trees each day as she passed by on her walk or going by in her carriage. He was sure the village boys would enjoy the horse chestnuts in autumn remembering his sister handing him a few horse chestnuts when he was very young and he liked the colour and the feel of the shiny objects so much he kept them until eventually he was made to throw them away.

The Baronet's thoughts were suddenly interrupted by the sight of a lone figure rushing down the lane and up the path to the church. He recognised her from the small cottages up the lane. She looked distressed as she pulled her shawl closer around her thin bony shoulders and passing him by he saw her slip into the church like a frightened animal. He stood there quietly and soon with head bowed, she reappeared, stopping for a moment to glance around her as if she didn't want anyone to see but catching sight of the Baronet, she quickly pulled her shawl tightly up over her bowed head and hastened on down the path.

He suddenly remembered this was the day the church bell would signal the start of the gleaning of the fields. The poor woman must have slipped up to the church for some reason before the gleaning work began; she looked so pale, thin and tired that he could not get her out of his mind. Her husband was one of the few men to return to the village after the battle of Waterloo, he returned not only with wounds but with some sort of illness affecting his lungs from which he had never really recovered.

He remembered many men returned to villages after the war with not only wounds but various types of disease. Many were too weak to work in the fields or anywhere else, some too weak to even survive. He wondered was this why the poor woman was driven to seek comfort or guidance in the church so early in the morning? He was sure she probably did most of the work to support the family like many other women, perhaps with the help of her children.

He tried to imagine life inside the dark, cramped cottages, they all looked too small and dismal to him and he knew many were rotten and damp inside. He was glad he had already started to replace and improve them with stronger stone buildings. His wife believed children should have some schooling and he agreed wondering what the children's lives were really like. He had given it all serious thought and he decided to build a school for the younger children, he knew his tender-hearted wife would be more than happy with his decisions. Being a gentle woman, she agreed with him wholeheartedly to help the village and had already asked him for extra grain to be distributed to the poorest families in need.

The church bell suddenly rang out making him jump and he saw the families starting to head down the lane towards the fields. The last sheaves of corn had been removed and the villagers were now allowed to search through the fields for any of the leftovers. The bell was the signal for the gleaning of the fields to begin.

Once the signal was given, there was usually a rush to be first. The youngest raced along together, laughing and calling to each other, whilst the older and wisest always took their time, they knew they must pace themselves for the long day's back breaking work ahead.

The woman married her young farm worker and settled in the village when no more than a girl. She was from over the valley and always dreamt one day her man would perhaps have some land to work, maybe own a pig or a few sheep but he had suddenly been forced into Wellington's army, there had been no way out. How she hated the war and the army and cursed the day they took him away. When he returned home, he was continually coughing and sometimes so bad he could barely get his breath.

On good days, her husband struggled to get into the fields to work but today was not a good day and feeling low in spirit, she thought if it hadn't been for the mistress who ordered bread to be distributed to the poorest in the village, they would have starved long since.

After the war, few men returned home to the villages without some injury or like her Thomas returned with the coughing sickness, some dying soon after in the cold damp conditions of their dwellings. When the Duke of Wellington returned to England, they all said he was a hero; everyone had been happy the war was over but now a few years had gone by and there was a feeling of unrest amongst the men. Some villages were already up in arms, food was so scarce and the costs rising higher and higher. There was harsh talk amongst the men and the women nervously wondered what was going to happen next.

She began to feel sick in the mornings; she tried to ignore it and did not say a word to anyone. She hoped it was not what she thought it was, for another mouth to feed would be a disaster. She already had problems trying to share the little food they had amongst the children. Upset and worried, she became desperate and went to the only place she knew to ask for help. What could she do, only throw herself on God's mercy. She tried hard to push away her feelings of not wanting another child, saying to herself if there was a baby, so be it, it was surely God's will and she must be thankful.

Although she felt desperate sometimes, she believed the master was going to make life better for them having heard all the gossip going around the village. She knew he had already made his men start to build new dry cottages and maybe her family could move to one, then her man would then get better and she prayed to God it would happen. Closing her eyes for a moment surrounded by the silence, she suddenly felt a slight surge of hope. As she hastily left the church, she glanced up at the stone head above the window, she always felt it was there to watch over them.

The sharpness of the early morning caused her to pull her shawl tighter as she stood for a moment in the quiet, feeling calmer. Suddenly, she caught sight of the master standing on the hilltop and feeling awkward she pulled the shawl up over her head and lowering her eyes hurried past him down the hill ready to set off to the fields.

She headed quickly to join her children; although she knew she would be too tired to stand up straight by the end of the day, it was vital for them to have the gleanings for grinding to make extra bread. Her two older children, a boy and a girl helped her as much as they could with the work whilst her younger daughter mainly looked after a little boy barely old enough to walk; he clung to his sister, already pathetically wailing in the sharp wind. She beckoned to them; they must make haste and catch up with the others, the day was just beginning, they must gather as much leftover grain as they could. She suddenly wished she could be back up on the hill where it was quiet, where she felt at peace.

*

Tom noticed the leaves beginning to change and there was that slight unmistakable smell of autumn in the air. It won't be long before the horse chestnuts fall to the ground, he cheerfully thought. The youngsters would be rummaging around under the old trees collecting the best of the shiny brown, plump conkers exactly as he and William did when they were boys.

He smiled to himself as the conker championships of his childhood came to mind. They had to be super specimens for the challenge, he and William used to dry them by the fire overnight to harden them off before putting the string through, some boys soaked them in vinegar first and some never let on the secrets of their most successful conkers. They all spent days looking for perfect horse chestnuts under the large trees on the green. They never did discover how scruffy young Jim from the back lane always managed to win with the puny conkers he used to use.

Tom laughed out-loud and thought he would go and have a chat to Ted about those long lost days and then with a sinking heart remembered Ted had gone. Liz came into the kitchen where he was sitting, saw his crest fallen face and suggested he went for a bit of a walk whilst it was dry to make him feel better.

"Aye, where's my wheels?"

Standing by the pond opposite Ted's garden, watching the ducks frantically paddling towards him, Tom felt downcast once again. Ted's garden was empty, no one working there, no cheery banter from his friend. Tom knew although his own family cared and were good to him, Ted like Nell was nearer his own age, someone who remembered those distant days just as he did; now he'd gone. Resigning himself, he continued on his way up the path leading to the church grounds. As he passed the tower on his way to stand on the hilltop, Tom stopped and looked up above the loophole window thinking at least his knight was always there.

Tom staggered on towards his favourite spot on the brow of the hill but somehow, it began to be a real effort to move even with his wheels. Feeling strange, he made his way back to the seat at the side of the porch and sinking down onto it, he wondered if he would ever be able to get up again and shut his eyes for a moment, his head drooped and his legs felt funny. He came to the decision he would just have to stay there until somebody came by who could give him a hand to get home.

He tried to take his mind off how he felt by remembering all the different families he knew still living in the village but somehow his mind couldn't concentrate and he just stared down at the grass to the side of him. Suddenly, his eyes focused on a couple of old stone steps half hidden there at the side of the seat and he tried hard to think why they were there. He knew there was once a flight of steps going up the side of the church wall going up to the narrow door leading into the church gallery. They turned the doorway into a window when they took the wooden gallery down.

You could still see the large iron hinges at the side of the window inside the church where the door had once hung. They said the gallery was where the workers sat but it had been taken down as it became unsafe and the steps were removed from the side of the wall leaving a few ugly marks. He tried to imagine what the church would have looked like with a wooden gallery at the back but he couldn't really think.

Still feeling strange, Tom continued to wait and suddenly, he heard young voices getting nearer. He was relieved to see his great grandsons Mark and Alex who came bounding up the path waving to him as they recognised him.

"I need a bit of help, lads, I can't get up." His voice sounded slow and unclear.

Mark looked at Tom. "I'll go and get Granddad Owen, shall I?"

"Aye, good lad. I'm getting cold." Tom tried to smile.

Mark bounded off and Alex sat down with Tom and looked at him. Tom tried to pat his arm gently telling him everything was fine, his old legs just wouldn't work properly.

"You're not going to die, are you, Granddad Tom?"

"No boy, course not, not yet, anyway if I did I'd not be far away, only here on the hill with the knight, I'd be keeping him company, sitting here on my seat." He tried once again to give a smile of reassurance as Alex looked up at the knight's head.

"Oh yes, that's good," Alex replied seriously thinking about it.

Owen and Mark arrived running up the path with Kath following behind.

"Just get me home, no hospital." He was adamant. "I just need a bit of help; my legs won't work today, no strength." Kathy sat with Tom while Owen reversed the car up the steep church driveway and together they struggled to get Tom into the front seat.

"We'll get the doctor to look you over as soon as we get you home."

"What for, I don't need one, I know what it is." He felt all agitated. "Just get me back home."

Sitting by his fire with his feet up, Tom's thoughts were glum. He knew vaguely what was wrong and although resigned to the inevitable the worst bit was realising he would not be able to go far under his own steam. He did allow them to send for the doctor with as good a grace as he could muster. There was no point in really making a fuss, it wouldn't help but he refused point blank to go to hospital telling the doctor he knew what it was; he was old and plain worn out.

Tom agreed after a bit of persuasion to let the doctor take blood samples to do some tests but he made it clear he didn't want to know any of the results and that was that. He would face whatever he had to in his own way. The doctor nodded and let it be but insisted that he must be very quiet for the next few days and rest up, preferably in bed.

Tom felt much better after a week of rest and even managed using his wheeler to walk to the back door for some fresh air; he stood there for a couple of minutes planning as soon as he could he would be going out for a bit of exercise.

The next day, Tom sat watching the fire crackling cheerfully as Liz popped her head around the door to ask him if he wanted anything. He said no he was fine and he was going to try having a walk down the lane to the seat by the pond. She looked a bit dubious but he was determined he wanted to try. He set off with Rosie close by his side and as soon as he passed through the gate, Liz rang Owen.

Owen and Alex found Tom sitting down on the bench by the pond, his hands resting on his wheeler in front of him, his eyes shut. Rosie was lying down by his feet and Alex sat down beside him to wait for him to wake up. Owen left them together whilst he went back where he'd parked the car to take Tom back home.

Tom opened his eyes and was pleased to see the boy, he wanted to know where Mark was and Alex told him he'd gone with their dad, a steam engine enthusiast and volunteer at the old The volunteers ran the old steam engine with its renovated carriages along a four mile section of track. It was a great attraction and the boys took it in turns to go with him when he went.

The thought of steam trains brought a gleam to Tom's eyes. He remembered the days when the steam train used to pass through the valley winding its way up to the mills and quarries further north; he could hear the sound it made and see the white smoke billowing out behind, he remembered it all so clearly.

Back at the farmhouse, Alex lay by the fire next to Rosie waiting for Owen who had gone to speak to Maggie and Liz. He gently stroked the old dog's soft fur and she looked up at Alex before quickly turning her head to check on Tom. Tom who had dropped off again suddenly opened his eyes and asked Alex what he had been up to before he came to see him.

"We've been playing a new game we've got. I can bring the game with me tomorrow when I visit if you like." Alex was always willing to share.

Tom laughed. "Aye, come down anytime but I won't be any good at your game, I'm too slow." He stopped to catch his breath. "Anyway, Joe's coming to have a clear up of the garden; he'll be lifting the last of the potatoes for your Aunt Maggie. You can help if you like," Tom went on. "When I was a boy, we always had lots of work to do in autumn getting ready for the winter months. We sometimes used to help the thatcher with the straw as they thatched the hayricks in those days."

"Did they? What did you have to do?"

"We had to make sure the straw was damp enough, watering it from a bucket. They said if it wasn't damp enough, it wouldn't lie and if we did it wrong, we copped it."

Alex looked up enthusiastically. "I might be a farmer when I get older and I could have a big farm in Australia with hundreds of sheep."

Pleased, Tom replied, "Aye, good idea. I always wanted to be a farmer just like my dad and my grandfather; we all wanted to be farmers. I never wanted to be anything else." And he beamed at Alex; he liked to think the boy was interested in farm work even in Australia.

The next morning, the sun came out looking very promising. When it warmed up a little, Tom sat outside near the backdoor where he could chat to Joe as he worked.

"Will you call me if you're cold?" Liz had her 'schoolmarm' face on and Tom nodded to his daughter and thought grumpily anything for peace.

"Morning, Joe," he called. "How are you?"

"Not bad, Tom. Potatoes still look good." He held some up for Tom to see just as Alex bounded around the corner shouting, "I've come to help, like I said." Rosie and Jess who were lying by the door ran over to him straight away happy to see him.

"Right then, Alex," said Joe, "get that sack and start to fill it with the potatoes. Make sure you knock the soil off first, okay?" Alex started work with enthusiasm.

"You ask Joe to show you the pumpkin he's growing for Harvest Festival. It'll look grand in the centre of the display." Tom gave a laugh to himself. It was a beauty, not a blemish on it and he almost felt envious. He watched the pair of them as they got stuck into the work and looking up noticed the birds wheeling about overhead. *It's going to get colder,* he thought. The house martins had already disappeared until spring and the year was definitely winding down, everything was getting ready.

Tom sat contentedly and looked over to Alex working alongside Joe, he saw the mop of red-gold hair bobbing about, straight away he thought of Owen at the same age working with his mother, he could see Meg showing him how to plant something or other and he remembered the two heads together, the exact same colour.

Tom's eyes closed and he saw Meg clear as day coming towards him as he stood on the hill. It was the day he knew with a sinking heart what she was about to tell him. He remembered his feeling of dismay and how many excuses flew into his mind until he saw how scared she looked; her eyes wide, looking up into his face and: he knew what he had to do. He remembered taking her shaking hands and

140

holding them tightly. Saying nothing, he tenderly drew her to him and after they were married, it took time but slowly, it dawned on him he was more than content, he was happy and although Nell would always be his close friend, it was Meg he loved.

By the time Nell and Jack were married and had their daughter Tess, Tom and Meg already had two children of his own and one more on the way. The day Meg told him she was expecting their second child, he had been so proud and if everything went to plan, he was about to take on the farm as a tenant farmer and then to top it all a third child. They were a real family and although their rewards in terms of money were minimal, somehow they always had enough.

His old heart jumped a little as he opened his eyes wondering where the years had gone. Feeling cold, he suddenly shivered and called to Alex.

"Can you get your Aunt Liz or Maggie?"

Liz hurried outside concerned. "Are you getting cold, Tom?"

"Aye, I'll come in now for a warm." Tom looked tired and she called Maggie to help.

Once inside sitting by his fire, he thought of Nell and smiled, she had a habit of popping into his mind on odd occasions when he least expected it. They had known each other for so long, well over eighty odd years in fact. It seemed like forever. Since the death of Meg and then Jack, he and Nell had grown even closer, in fact over the last ten years they had grown more alike, Nell always told him they were growing plain old and cantankerous together.

Looking into his room ten minutes later, Liz found him once again asleep, his head sunk on his chest and she felt a little fearful and sad as she watched him, he was getting to look so frail. The wood on the fire crackled sending sparks up the chimney and as she caught a whiff of the smoke from the burning logs, the familiar smell somehow soothed her agitated feelings. For now, nothing had changed all was well and she went out of the room closing the door softly behind her.

Tom was walking along the old railway line that used to run from the tiny station a few miles away through the village. He followed behind the slow steam engine along the track for what seemed like miles until suddenly it disappeared into the old brick tunnel and he was left standing miraculously on the hilltop in front of the tower although he knew, the old brick tunnel was more than a mile odd away from the hill.

The railway line had long been dismantled and these days the pathway under the trees was constantly used by ramblers and hikers searching for the great outdoors. A car parking area replaced the tiny station and in summer, there was no peace from the never ending visitors walking or cycling along the track.

Most of the cottages were built nearly two hundred years ago and the many visitors were always happily peering over garden walls and gateways, through open windows and doorways as if eager to try and catch a glimpse of the past. Muttering loudly in his sleep, he opened his eyes a little and heard the fire crackling in the grate.

There was a knock and opening his eyes struggling to focus he saw Kath pop her head around the door. "I've some family news, Tom, and I've come to tell you." She beamed happily at him somehow looking younger. She went on,

"You will never guess." She paused. "Jen is coming home, she is going to work in the hospital down in the town and she's hoping to rent a cottage in the village." Kath was all smiles. Tom stared at her and his eyes lit up. "I knew it, I knew it. Does Glyn know? Wait 'til I see Nell."

"Now, Tom, don't go reading too much into it. She and Glyn haven't seen much of each other lately. And…" She paused. "There is more news." She looked at him before taking a breath.

"Laura is expecting another baby."

He looked at Kath a bit concerned. "Will it be all right? Alex is nearly seven."

"Of course, Tom, she's still young enough and pretty healthy."

Laughing, Kath leant over and kissed his cheek. "Everything will be fine, Tom."

That night, Tom lay in bed thinking of the news. He was to have another great grandchild and Jen was coming home. He remembered when Jen and Glyn had been seeing each other regularly he and Nell had felt the same, excited, they both had such hopes but when she left the area to work down south and Glyn went quiet, it was all a big disappointment. He and Nell wanted the same thing, for some reason they knew it would make things right. The two of them should be wed and there was still time for them to have children, maybe this time it would happen before it was too late. Tom couldn't wait to see Nell. Jen was coming home.

After a couple of weeks, Tom began to feel stronger, resting had helped and he wanted to get outside in the fresh air, to go for his walk to the hilltop on his own, just to go and sit on the seat near the knight. He couldn't wait; maybe he could get Owen to buy him a different set of wheels: one with a seat to sit on if he got tired.

As he explored the different possibilities, he felt optimistic and believed everything was going to be all right. Soon, he'd be up on his hill standing in front of the tower where he wanted to be, listening to the sound of the yews rustling in the breeze or watching the grass as it rippled across the hill. He couldn't wait to be up there sitting near the carved head of his knight. He wanted to feel the cool breeze on his face and suddenly a surge of excitement and anticipation crept over him and he felt some life begin to flow back into his old body. He suddenly felt he was still alive and he couldn't wait to go to his hill.

*

VIII

The news headlines read 'Germany invades Belgium' and 'Asquith declares War on the Invaders'. Everyone said the war would not last long; it would be over very quickly once the British troops were deployed. He sniffed, he was not convinced.

Sir James stood on the hill in front of the tower and pondered his own problems. He had not been well over the past couple of years and he knew the estate would soon have to be run by his sons. Originally, his wish was for all of them to share the responsibility but his oldest was already an officer in the British Army and with a feeling of despondency at the breaking news, Sir James quickly realised he would be one of the first to be sent into action.

His second son was out prospecting in South Africa trying to make his fortune in diamonds and he hadn't heard from him for nearly a year; he would take some finding. Sir James was therefore thankful his third son Henry, the steadiest, could be relied upon. The only trouble was he too might be called upon at any time to do his duty in the army. His fourth son Edward by his second wife was very young a child, only seven years old.

The Baronet walked thoughtfully and carefully around the church past the tower oblivious of the carved knight above the window who stared over his head towards the yews. Sir James stopped in front of the solid door and, as he always did, ran his hands over the worn pillars each side.

Lifting the heavy latch, the door creaked and groaned as it slowly opened and he stepped inside the dim musty smelling interior. Walking towards the chancel arch thinking of his sons, he stood looking at the stained glass window above the altar. After a few minutes, he wandered over to the brass commemorative plaques on the wall nearby and stepped closer to read one of the inscriptions. He read one of his distant relatives, a captain, was killed in the Crimean War and it struck him how young the poor officer was. Young men always went off excitedly to war before getting killed. Thinking once again of his sons, he sighed deeply and stood quietly for a few moments before going back outside into the fresh air. Wandering to the brow of the hill, he stood looking over the land below for a few moments until the harsh sound of the rooks penetrated his subconscious. He shivered deciding he was getting cold and quickly set off down the path.

The young farmhand walked smartly through the old gateway onto the manor estate; he passed the lodge and headed down towards the village. He marched as if on parade, chipper and full of energy. He and his pals had been down to the first meeting in the town, the hall was jam packed and now he was proudly returning home one of the four who had immediately volunteered and signed up to join the army. He was going to fight for King and Country. They would show those Germans a thing or two when they got over there.

His pals had stayed in town but he wanted to get home to tell his girl and his family the news. He walked at a pace down the lane towards the large chestnut trees in front of the hill and stopped. It suddenly dawned on him it may not be quite so easy telling everyone. He slowly began to wonder how his mother would react when she heard what he'd done; his father would surely understand, be pleased even.

Doubts crept into Will's mind; he wondered how to tell them. How would his father really take the news? Anyway, it was too late now, he had done it, he couldn't back out and he had to go. At least, the four of them were going together. He lingered about under the trees wanting to think clearly about the best way to approach the subject with his folks. Looking at the hill, he suddenly raced up the path to the church grounds where it was quiet. He wandered slowly around reading the inscriptions on the family graves and spotted the worn stone of his great, great grandfather Thomas who returned home from the Battle of Waterloo to die a few years later with some lung complaint. The family always proudly mentioned him; he was famous, he actually fought against Napoleon Bonaparte but his poor great, great grandmother or so the story went, died a few years later, they said in hushed voices she was just plain worn out.

William continued to wander around the church grounds and suddenly stopped in front of a large headstone near to the base of the Saxon Cross. He knew the family well; their son had gone off to sea to work on the Titanic. He remembered how the whole village had been in awe, someone they actually knew going on that first voyage and

147

many of the lads were more than envious. It seemed like yesterday, no one ever thought that great ship would sink. Not the Titanic. He remembered the chap well and when the disaster happened, like the others in the village he could not believe he'd gone down with the ship, actually drowned. There was talk the family had decided they would eventually add his name to the family gravestone.

They told the young recruits when they signed up they were going to the large army barracks a few miles away for training before being sent away and Will felt reassured the four of them were going together. He had never been to sea and just heard stories about storms and high waves from those who had actually ventured on the water. He hoped when the time came, it would be a good crossing and in a reasonable frame of mind decided to go and tell his older brother the news first before going home, then he would go to see his girl later that evening and ask her to wait for him. Passing the church porch, he stopped and hesitatingly made his way to the heavy door. Once inside the church, he thought maybe he would ask for a blessing, he might not get another chance.

The same old familiar smell hit him as he stepped through the doorway and he took off his cap and quietly walked up the aisle towards the carved oak rails in front of the altar. He stared up at the stained glass window above and not knowing quite what to say bowing his head, he repeated the Lord's Prayer. As he turned to go, a brass plaque caught his eye and he went over to have a closer look. The young officer died gallantly in action, he couldn't quite read where or when. They always put they die gallantly he thought and suddenly he hoped if he had to die, it would be in the same way, gallantly.

As he lifted the heavy iron latch, the door made the usual noise as the hinges needed oiling and he stepped out into the porch. Automatically, he ran his hands over the worn pillars each side of the door remembering the story of the English Bowmen. Passing the narrow window where the Knight's head stared into the distance, he stopped to look at it before continuing on his way thinking it was strange how all the village men seemed to end up fighting in France.

Will's older brother was already married with two young sons. He lived up past the manor and he found him working in his garden at the back of the cottage; he was busy cutting up a section of tree trunk into logs. All his wood was stacked neatly nearby ready for the winter. The men from the village could have all the fallen wood they wanted but they were not allowed to cut any tree down and everyone had a good stock of wood to last through the winter. The smell of wood smoke always reminded Will of home and the village.

Will watched his brother as he told him his news; Jack stopped work and slowly stood upright. Will looked at his solemn face and hurriedly told him not to worry. They would soon sort the problem out and be home. Jack shook his head and gave him a strange look then silently carried on with his task chopping wood. All he said was, "Have you told them yet?"

Will's mother sat motionless, pale and quiet whilst his father shouted angrily.

"You're a fool, our Will." As he glared at his youngest son.

"Why?" he went on. "Why are you in such a rush? It could go on for years and you're too young and they haven't called you up yet. Why?" His father was furious. "You're a bloody idiot." He turned his back on him and said in a hoarse whisper, "Go! Get out of my sight."

Will had not expected his father's reaction and he stormed out of the cottage before he said something to retaliate, something he would regret. He was almost as angry as his father. With gritted teeth, he quickly marched straight down the lane past the Manor and with nowhere else to go, went back up the hill. *They're all wrong*, he thought; *they think the war will go on for years, it won't, I know it won't.* His head was in a whirl and he thought anyway, *I've volunteered with the others; now I must go and get on with it. Why didn't anyone understand?*

For a long time, he just stood looking down from the hill until the wind picked up and he heard the old yews begin to creak. It was getting late and as the light began to fade, he felt in a calmer frame of mind. He wondered if his brother was still out in his garden working, he could go and tell him what happened, maybe ask him to talk to them, help to explain. He breathed in deeply, catching the smell of the evening mist as it drifted upwards. He saw it mingle with wisps of pale blue smoke from the chimneys in the village and a strange loneliness crept over him as he stood there. He could see his mother hunched over, probably crying and his father red in the face with anger. He was sorry. How could he make things okay; make everything all right, he would go home and try to make amends.

With renewed purpose, he walked quickly down the path towards the wooden gate and suddenly wondered if anything

150

happened to him, would he want to be brought back to the village, to the hill or be left wherever he fell, with his pals. Then shaking his head, he opened the gate.

"No, we'll all be marching home heroes. That's what we'll be...bloody heroes." And taking a deep breath, he pulled his shoulders back and with head high he marched up the lane.

*

The weather was perfect for autumn with crisp mornings, cool evenings and warm days. Tom sat looking out through the window at the familiar trees and hedges beginning to change colour. As the afternoon wore on, he became restless and began to wonder where Maggie and Liz had vanished to, it was very quiet, even Jess had disappeared. He decided to watch something on television, there might be snooker or gardening; it would while away the time.

These days, Tom couldn't concentrate for long and on many occasions just dropped off to sleep in the middle of a program. The news usually depressed him; the world seemed to be in constant turmoil. *Crazy people blowing up everything and everyone, would it ever stop?* Tom wondered if the world was going mad or would there be another war. He remembered the time his father told them about 'The Great War' and Uncle Will who marched off with three other lads from the village. They left for the 'War to end all Wars' and not one of them returned.

He decided not to bother with the television after all and grumbling softly to himself wished, as he always did, he could go out for a walk. He loved autumn with the smell of smoke from the chimneys and garden bonfires. To get up and move around the room was hard enough for him these days, he felt plain tired out most of the time. *Maybe I can go tomorrow,* he thought. *Aye, I'll get one of them to take me in the wheelchair.*

His dream of walking to the hill under his own steam had slowly disappeared and he just had to accept the fact he needed someone to help. He looked down at Rosie who was sleeping in front of the fire. "You want to go-a-walk. Don't you, girl?" The dog lifted her head at the word 'walk' and then sank back down as she realised Tom was not making a move.

He sat looking at his weather beaten hands resting on the arms of the chair, his knuckles large and lumpy; it must have been all those long years of work in icy cold weather he thought as he turned them over to look at the ingrained callouses still there as reminders of his hard working past.

It suddenly dawned on him where Maggie and Liz were, up at the church helping to decorate it ready for Harvest Festival. Joe had already wheeled his massive pumpkin up there on the wheelbarrow. He deliberately wheeled it past the window for Tom to have a look before he took it away. It was to be the centre piece taking pride of place amongst the other contributions of fruit and flowers. Tom could see it clearly in his mind surrounded by garden offerings, cabbages, carrots, potatoes, parsnips and onions. There would be plenty of apples and pears highly polished as well but he was sure Joe's pumpkin would look magnificent.

Tom thought fondly of his old friend Ted, every year Ted grew his beautiful bronze chrysanthemums for this occasion and he remembered the large blooms so well with their perfect inward curving petals. No doubt, there would be masses of flowers around the church windowsills and a big display on the wooden stand near the pulpit but Ted's chrysanthemums would be sorely missed by all who knew him.

Tomorrow was Saturday and Tom wondered if Owen or Joe would take him up to the church to have a look at the Harvest Festival display while it was quiet. He wouldn't be going to the Harvest supper to be held in the village hall on Saturday evening. He knew he wouldn't have the energy, although the spirit was willing. The supper would be followed by games and music as usual but he wasn't tempted and maybe Nell would come over. She hadn't been too well herself lately, she might like a bit of peace and quiet cosily sitting by the fire reminiscing with him.

"Tom!" called Nell. "Tom, where are you?" She staggered into the room using her two walking sticks. "It's getting to be a long way from the kitchen, or is it me?"

She gasped for breath as Tess following behind steered her to her favourite easy chair put next to Tom ready for her. Maggie stuck her head through the doorway as Tess helped her mother take her coat off before she sat down.

"We're off now. One of us will sort some supper for you a bit later, okay?"

"Aye, we'll be fine," Nell replied. "You all go and have a good time."

Maggie laughed as Tess mouthed the words behind Nell's back; 'And no getting drunk on the home made wine'. These days, Nell had various sayings for every occasion.

Later, Liz came over to see to supper and then left them to it. Although it looked good, Tom only picked at him, whilst Nell managed to finish most of hers and she looked at him with some concern.

"You're not feeling up too much, are you, Tom?"

He shook his head, and she noticed he looked pale. She felt uneasy remembering Tom as a tall, strong chap. She could see him standing in the garden that summer day with his sleeves rolled up, his muscular arms brown as berries. It was not long after he and Meg were married, before Owen was born. They were chatting to William who was waiting for her standing by the stonewall that separated their gardens. Meg stood waving to Nell as she approached and Nell remembered, although she would never admit it, she was suddenly jealous. She was Tom's oldest friend, not Meg.

"What's the matter, Nell? You thinking of the past?" Tom looked at her and she lowered her eyes as he took her old, veined hand in his. "What is it?"

"I was just thinking of us all when we were young and how jealous I was of Meg and you together. That part of life has gone by so quickly, Tom. When did we get so old?"

"We've still a bit longer to go, Nell, but I've told Owen when my time does come I want everyone to see me out up at the pub. No weeping and wailing, just lots of music and merrymaking. Okay?" He looked right at her. "There's to being no weeping everywhere!" Tom went on, "I'm ready, or as ready as I ever will be." He paused for a few moments, adding, "Although we're bound to miss whoever goes first, Nell. We've been friends for such a long time, always part of each other's life. Meg and your Jack both knew how close we were and we always will be."

He saw a tear suddenly drop onto her lap and he clasped her hand tightly.

"Don't cry, Nell." He paused and then gave a laugh. "And thank God no one is here to see us getting all soppy. She nodded and despite herself smiled."

"Aye, I suppose so. Tom, you're an old rascal but you know how I feel, I'll always love you." She went on. "Maybe we should have got together." Then she gave a chuckle as she looked up into his old red-rimmed eyes and shook her head adding, "No perhaps not, I'd have made you miserable and you would have driven me mad and I know you were really meant for, Meg." She sighed before going on. "Oh well, we make great friends." She stopped. "No, we're more than that, aren't we?"

"Aye, always," he replied as they sat there holding hands by the fire together.

Nell thought about telling Tom what really did happen between her and William. She remembered asking William to marry her, how shocked he looked as he refused, almost horrified. He looked right at her and said he didn't want to marry anyone, he wanted to be free to have some adventure and he wasn't the marrying kind and she had been livid.

Tom interrupted her thoughts by suddenly asking, "What do you think then about Jen returning? I'm hoping she and Glyn will get back together, make a go of it."

Forgetting the past, Nell brightened up. "I'm sure it will happen sooner or later, I think it's meant to be. If you pop off before me, Tom, I suppose I'll have to stay to check they do make a go of it."

"Aye." Tom started to yawn, suddenly feeling tired and his eyes began to close and as usual his head slowly sank down onto his chest.

"What did you mean you're ready?" asked Nell waking him up. He wearily opened his eyes for a moment.

"I'm ready because I know where I'm going, like I told young Alex, I shan't be going far away, just up on the hill with everyone else."

Nell nodded and laughed. "You'd better all wait for me then, our Tom. All of you, or else!"

One afternoon, waiting for Liz to return from town, Tom felt strangely agitated because he couldn't go out for his walk any more. He missed the sight of the pond as he headed up to the church to stand on the hill looking out towards the horizon. He knew many folks went up on there to stretch their legs or to look at the ancient buildings or gravestones but for him the hill was different, the hill was special; he always felt he somehow belonged to it; it was home.

He remembered the church so clearly: he could see every stone in the tower with the narrow loophole window and the carved head of the knight staring towards the yew trees opposite. He saw the church door with the carved stone above the pillars. He could even see the base of the Saxon Cross hidden amongst the long grass by the wall and he could feel the wind blowing across the hillside soothing the spirit. He remembered when it blew from the north it roared straight down the valley and you could feel its power as it rocked the sturdy yew trees.

Shutting his eyes, he saw inside the church, the carved altar rails, the large dark oak pulpit and the beautiful stained glass windows. He could see the font near the door and the simple chancel arch with the large family memorial at the side. He even remembered the brass plaques around the walls especially the one to honour the four men from the village including Uncle Will who lost their lives in the First World War.

The light began to fade and Tom in a reflective mood sat and wondered when Liz or Maggie would come home, he wished they would hurry up. He sat by the glow of the fire staring into it whilst Rosie slept contentedly at his feet and feeling a little melancholy, he waited patiently for either of them to return.

The rest of October was a blur of golden colour with sunshine right up to the last few days when the skies turned heavy and grey. The birds outside Tom's window were busy feasting on fat scraps off the bird table; they made a noise as they scrambled to eat as much as possible. Maggie and Liz were hard pressed to keep them going. Joe called in most days to tell Tom what was going on in the garden and, sometimes they would get the dominoes out for a game to keep their spirits up.

The wind started to blow the leaves off the trees as winter approached and the clocks went back the usual hour as the nights drew in. Tom sat by his fire as if quietly waiting and he often dreamt of the past. He remembered Meg after they were first married how he watched her work and how she loved the garden, planting her vegetables filling the borders with flowers and she even sorted out a circular patch of meadow grass, growing wild flowers which she loved.

Along the dry stonewall dividing the garden from the field at the back, Meg got him to plant blackberries and wild roses to scramble over it. She was always planning and doing something besides making things for the children to wear and he noticed she took a pride in her work.

He sighed gently as he sat by the fire with his memories, Rosie close by his side. These days, Rosie never moved far from him and every so often she looked up as if to check on him and he stroked the soft fur on her head.

Tom seemed to remember the past better than events that happened yesterday. As he stared into the embers of the fire, he had a clear picture of William telling him he had joined up. He did it on the spur of the moment just like their Uncle Will and Tom knew straight away things would never be the same but there was nothing he or anyone could do about it. William's fate was sealed and although Tom had long ago come to terms with his brother's death, he still missed him after all these years and when thinking back to the days together in their youth, he felt a deep sense of loneliness.

At one time, Tom used to question his decision to stay behind on the farm during the conflict, not joining the army with William but continuing to do his job growing vital crops. Tom sighed and thought of his father who made the same decision, staying behind to work on the land while Uncle William marched off to war and he wondered how his father felt, he never heard him ever speak of it.

Nell's voice always came into his head loud and clear, telling him off, telling him someone had to stay behind to farm the land, grow the much needed grain and vegetables; help put food on the table. He suddenly thought of all the times he went and stood in front of the tower after long hard working days, unsure; did he do the right thing. He would go and stand on the hill and it never failed to help. He remembered how the silence surrounding him felt good and he would breathe in the cool, soothing air and soon he was ready to get off home.

*

IX

Sir Henry stood inside the church porch looking out, holding his stout wooden staff sheltered from the cold afternoon breeze, his retriever sat quietly by his side. It was late in the afternoon and the branches of the yew trees swayed back and fore making their familiar sound. They always reminded him of the ancient tree in his wood behind the hall, even if they were half the size. They had stood there he was sure, for a good many years opposite the church, come rain or shine and it pleased him to think they would probably still be there long after his day.

The Second World War now seemed years ago and preparations for the Coronation of Princess Elizabeth were well in hand. After the hardship of the war years and the death of the King, this was just what everyone needed; something to cheer about.

He remembered how shocked everyone felt when Edward abdicated for Mrs Simpson before the war and poor Bertie had to be crowned George the Sixth. He was always a shy man who found his royal duties more than difficult but there had been no option for him and when he died, Sir Henry like many others wondered had it all just been too much for him. Although he felt a deep sadness along with the rest of the nation when the King passed away, Henry firmly believed in the young Princess Elizabeth and looked forward to the future.

He peered out of the porch looking towards the small side gate and proudly thought of his newly built village hall erected just out of his sight on the spare ground by the snicket leading to the duck pond. He had long ago decided it would add to village life but he had put the idea on hold during the Second World War. Now at last the building was completed and nearly ready for use, just a few coats of paint needed to finish the job.

The Baronet known sometimes in the village as Sir Harry looked forward to the Coronation; he would have had a seat in Westminster Abbey and believed it was definitely a privilege to be able to be there but his health lately was not too good. With the war years far behind them, everyone was excited and talked of the new 'Elizabethan' age. The village was to be decorated with flags and there would be parties for the children. He smiled to himself; the women were well ahead with their plans and had sorted it all out. In the evening, there would be music and entertainment with everyone invited to the newly built village hall. The whole event got the village buzzing and he felt a surge of their optimism and excitement.

Everything had changed so much since the war, in the last year or two he had been ill and wondered about the future of the estate. He had no children of his own and knew the whole estate would eventually be passed to his much younger brother, Edward. He remembered his older brothers all killed in action long ago during the two World Wars and suddenly, he felt his age.

The modern world was ever a mystery to Sir Harry but he knew the time had arrived to make plans; the estate must bring in extra income to cover the rising costs of the upkeep. He would send for Edward who lived up on the borders of Scotland to come and discuss the problems before time slipped by and it was too late. As he stood on the brow of the hill with his dog close to heel, he watched a tall strong looking figure approach the hill.

Sir Harry recognised him immediately, he knew him well. It was his best tenant farmer who through the war years helped not only to complete the food quota for the government but gave him his loyalty one hundred percent. Sir Harry remembered the early days when he had just inherited the estate before the start of the war and was new to the running of it; he badly needed help and his man had not let him down. Food production had been top priority and before the land girls were brought in to help because of the shortage of working men. He remembered how every bit of green pastureland had to be ploughed up and planted and young Tom worked until he dropped.

Sir Harry suddenly remembered Tom's older brother William who joined the army right at the beginning of the War, he was one of the first to volunteer only to return to the village when badly wounded. He never really recovered and only survived for a couple of years after he returned. He remembered Tom had taken it hard. The story was, their Uncle Will did exactly the same thing in the First World War; he was also one of the first to volunteer along with three other young men from the village but not one of them returned home and Harry sadly thought of his own brothers and cleared his throat.

Tom walked quickly up the path so engrossed in his own thoughts he did not noticed Sir Harry standing in the shadows beneath the small window in the tower. Eventually when he spotted him, Tom raised his hand and nodded to him in greeting. Smiling, the Baronet beckoned him over and the retriever ran towards the farmer wagging his tail greeting him like a long lost friend.

"Have you seen the village hall now that the men have completed it, Tom?" Sir Harry signalled to his dog 'to heel' and the dog ran over and sat close to his master's side. He went on, "It should be ready for use soon, and it just needs a few coats of paint. I think the whole village will enjoy having a place to get together in."

"Aye, it will be appreciated." Tom gave a smile. "The women always wanted a village hall. They'll put it to good use especially with all the celebrations."

Satisfied, Sir Harry nodded. "I'm also going to put a good strong seat just here, this side of the porch, Tom; we could all do with a sit down sometimes." And they both laughed.

Together, they walked towards the brow of the hill where each of them had often stood on various occasions. Harry wondered what his next project would be now the hall was finished and he asked Tom what he thought. Tom looked towards the tree-lined avenue leading to the main road and reminded him about the time he had mentioned replacing all the old trees with new saplings. The original trees were old, some had been struck by lightning and begun to rot and decay, their poor split trunks stood there looking a little pathetic, only a few decent branches left, they definitely needed replacing.

Sir Harry nodded and decided to go and make a few enquiries. He would get the men started on the job. He bid Tom farewell and limped as quickly as he could down the path with his dog following close behind. Tom watched him from the hill and remembered him as a younger, stronger man before all his medical difficulties and problems. He had a lot of respect and time for Sir Harry who could work as well as any man he knew and he watched his dogged determination as he painfully walked as quick as he could over the gravelled area around the side of the Manor Hall.

The afternoon light began to fade, the day had gone well and Tom was in a good mood. He set off towards the farm to complete what he needed to do for the evening. Although he loved to stand on the hilltop looking out over the land, he knew he must go and finish his day's work.

Heading around the tower on his way towards the side gate, he passed the carved head of the Knight above the window. Glancing up at it, Tom greeted it with a nod.

"Aye, a seat just here would be good," he said out-loud. "I can sit a few minutes." He laughed as he looked up at the Knight's head. "And have a chat."

*

Tom leant forward in his chair trying to ease his back. It was an overcast dismal grey day not quite raining but not dry, the air full of moisture and he looked through the window at the sky and thought 'No butterflies! No bees! No birds! No leaves! November'. He'd heard the words somewhere, a poem or a song but he wasn't sure where. Tom always loved November, a mysterious month with misty mornings and the strong smell of smoke as the villagers kept themselves warm and cheerful by stoking up the fires.

Bonfire night had already come and gone, Tom had sat in comfort with Rosie and Jess asleep at his feet. Maggie had gone with Kath and Owen to watch the firework display but Liz stayed at home in the kitchen baking, she certainly didn't fancy an evening out in the cold. The sound of fireworks in the distance caused the dogs to raise their heads; ears alert, but in general, it had been reasonably quiet at the back of the farmhouse in Tom's room.

Remembering other bonfire nights Tom could almost see the large well-built bonfire in the corner of the field and wondered how many guys there were. He had forgotten to ask. There always used to be a competition years ago held before the fireworks began. The guys were proudly wheeled around in a circle in decorated wheelbarrows for the judges, who took their time to make their decision. Eventually, the best one was declared the winner and had the dubious pleasure of being first on the bonfire; a bit of a gruesome practise, he thought.

When Owen and the girls were young, there were not many fancy fireworks like today but Tom remembered the time Owen and the other lads poked about the smouldering ashes of the burnt out bonfire the next day, looking for this or that. Their arms, legs and clothes were soon black and sooty. He remembered Meg marching Owen inside with vague threats of having to stay in for the rest of the day if he didn't get cleaned up straight away. He could only go back outside to play if he kept away from any fires lit or otherwise. Afterwards, Tom confided to Meg with a grin, he had similar sort of experiences when he was young, but got a wallop off his father. *Aye*, he thought, *we were the same, getting black and grimy, getting into hot water.*

As he sat half asleep, he saw himself as a young farmer going out at this time of year in all weather, even when early sunrise sent streaks of vivid red across the sky, a sign of bad weather to come, 'shepherds warning'. He still enjoyed the start of any new day in autumn, whatever was thrown at him. He loved it all, especially the still misty days when the leaves fell silently from the trees one by one and he watched them float slowly, silently, to the ground.

Tom thought of Meg how they used to stroll up on the hill with the scent of wood smoke from bonfires and chimneys rising up into the air. Together, they stood by the tower sheltered from the cold and he thought of her warm sweet smelling body close to his, arousing his passion. He looked up at the mantelpiece to his precious photographs, his failing eyes searched out the small photograph she had given him when she was young, now in the heavy ornate silver frame. It was always his favourite, she was not deemed a beauty but there was something about her; the large warm eyes and he suddenly thought of that first time he looked right into them. He stared into the glowing fire beneath the mantelpiece and whispered hoarsely. "Megan, do you remember girl, do you remember?" He had not called her that for years. Her mother always called her Megan but she preferred to be called plain Meg it was simpler.

Tom suddenly heard the birds making an infernal row and automatically looked towards the window, he couldn't see them but he knew they were squabbling over the titbits on the bird table. *Must be the magpies*, he thought and his eyes heavy with sudden weariness started to close, his head sank and he could vaguely hear the noise outside until it suddenly stopped and the only sound was the fire crackling in the grate.

Next morning was clear and there was a heavy frost, Tom's spirits lifted, he felt cheerful seeing the bright sun. There was a knock on Tom's door and Joe popped his head around.

"I wondered if you wanted to come out in the wheelchair for a bit of fresh air, Tom."

"Aye," Tom replied enthusiastically. "Can we go up on the hill?" And Joe nodded. Liz was in the kitchen and insisted not only must Tom wear his warm coat but have the rug over his knees as well. "Not too long, Joe. It's sharp cold outside today."

"We won't be long," Joe replied.

Tom started to grumble under his breath as Joe pushed the wheelchair out through the gate. He was all wrapped up much to his annoyance, the rug tucked around him. Like a bloody child he thought. They set off down the lane and he soon stopped muttering about women in general and pointed to the trees still hanging with frost.

"Look, Joe, that's a sight." Joe nodded as he manoeuvred the wheelchair up the path past the village hall to the side gate. Tom suddenly thought of old Sir Harry, how the estate went to his younger brother Edward and some years ago, Sir Edward's son, Ned, took over the estate along with the title. Tom liked and got on well with each of them in turn but he did miss old Sir Harry remembering how they worked side by side during the war years.

The side gate to the church grounds was only just wide enough for Tom's wheelchair but Joe managed to get Tom through it and going past the porch with some effort they headed towards the brow of the hill and Tom felt the usual surge of anticipation he always felt. He looked up at the Knight's head as they passed; he had missed his old friend. They soon stood in front of the tower looking down over the Hall. "It's still a grand sight," Tom muttered as he looked up at Joe.

"Aye," said Joe. "But times are changing Tom, anything could happen at any time." He looked at Tom's crestfallen face and felt a bit ashamed.

"Take no notice of me, Tom: I had a real bad night last night, couldn't sleep and was restless even when I did drop off." He stopped for a few moments and went on. "I kept turning everything over in my mind." Joe gazed out over the land. "Sometimes, Tom, you can't forget." He swallowed hard and lowered his voice. "I sometimes can't forgive myself, I keep thinking I should have been there Tom...at home with her...spent more time..." He sighed deeply.

"It wasn't your fault, Joe. You had to work, or how else would you manage to survive, and pay your way. You weren't to know."

Joe nodded and stared into the distance. "Aye but it's still hard to forgive yourself."

"I know and we all have to come to terms with some things," Tom went on. "We all have our demons. Mine was I never went to fight alongside my brother William in the last war."

"Why not then?" Joe put his hand on Tom's shoulder.

"Because I knew I couldn't leave with everyone depending on me to help keep growing food. There was no one else to really pull the work in." He sighed. "It was a hard choice and I heard plenty of whispered comments by some and I began to doubt myself. I wondered was I right, did I make the right decision or was I just plain afraid to go."

Joe looked down at him. "No, I know you weren't afraid, Tom. You just did what you knew you had to do and got on with it."

"Aye but I was afraid in some ways, Joe, afraid of what others would say if I stayed, but I knew someone had to stay and work the fields. I couldn't bring myself to talk about it, not even to Meg. When William came home badly wounded, I was so cut up. I kept thinking if I'd only joined up when he did, maybe…" His voice trailed off.

After a while, Tom continued, "One afternoon, I just told him how bad I felt, how I wished I had joined up at the same time, been with him. He looked at me for a long while before shaking his head, telling me not to be so daft. He said I could have ended up just like him or worse and he looked straight at me and I remember his exact words."

"It was all madness, the slaughter, the destruction, everything; all those poor bodies; theirs and ours. He stopped and I remember his face looked drained of any colour before he continued saying. At least, you were growing food for everyone at home; you were helping keep them alive."

Tom stood there staring into the distance before adding, "I thought about those words many times, Joe."

Each of them fell silent for a while until Joe suddenly shivered. "Come on, Tom, let's get off home to the warm. It's getting cold and Liz will wonder where we are."

That night, Maggie found Tom in a quiet mood when she popped in to see to the fire. "Are you all right, Dad?" she asked.

"Aye, just thinking," he answered.

He had been thinking of William and the war, when Uncle Will came into his mind. When they were boys every year, they went with their father to the Remembrance Service in November down at the cenotaph in the town. As a boy, Tom watched his father put his wooden cross with the poppy alongside all the others. He remembered standing there next to William in the bitter cold as the bugler played the 'Last Post' a haunting sound. As a child, he had no real understanding of war but as he sat there he thought of all those men who died, including his brother William who didn't survive for long. It filled him with a feeling of emptiness, so many wasted lives.

He rarely mentioned the war years these days and there was only Nell left in the village who remembered back so far. He sank back in his chair as he looked up towards a faded photograph of William and himself standing together just before he left for France and once again, he thought. If only…and suddenly, the old man's eyes filled up.

The next morning, Kathy brought down some gardening magazines for Tom to look at; her cheeks were glowing pink from the walk. He had just settled himself in his easy chair and she noticed he was a bit pale and his blue veined hands looked delicate as they rested on the arms of the chair. She cheered up as she told him Laura and Ben had decided if their new baby was a girl, they would call her Megan after Grandma Meg. Tom was pleased and smiled. "A good name, Megan."

Kath continued, "Liz has asked Joe to come for Christmas as he's on his own." Tom nodded and smiled. "I often wonder if Joe and Liz are…you know…"

"No, I don't think so, Tom, Liz is quite a bit older than Joe, I think she just likes having a younger man to look after, to fuss over and I think he enjoys being pampered."

"Aye, you could be right. He's not been happy lately living in the cottage on his own and he told me his lease is up soon." Tom looked a bit concerned. "I hope he doesn't want to leave the village. I would miss him, Kath."

He wondered what would happen if Joe did leave; he really would miss him if he went anywhere else to live. They had become good friends and Joe always cheered him up. Who else would talk about gardening with him now Ted had gone? Tom just didn't want him to go and he forgot Kath was still there until suddenly she said.

"Maybe Joe could rent here at the farm until he perhaps makes his mind up what he wants to do, there's the big spare bedroom upstairs that used to be yours and it would be a big help for all of you. We can ask Liz and Maggie what they think, I'm sure they won't mind. They've been thinking about finding a lodger for a while to help with the rent." Tom perked up, maybe Joe would come and live at the farm and suddenly he felt optimistic.

After Kath left, Tom watched the flames dancing in the fire and listened to the wood crackling and dozed off. He saw himself walking down towards the duck pond, crossing over the lane and up the path by the side of the village hall.

171

He jauntily went past Ted's cottage and he could see the back of his old friend bending over working in the garden. He called Ted's name but Ted went on working until eventually he slowly turned and waved and Tom happily continued on towards the church gate.

Going into the grounds past the church porch, he saw himself as strong as any young man, walking without a stick and he stood for a few moments in front of the Knight's head, the carved features staring out as always. He made his way to the brow of the hill where he stood looking over the fields below and wondered why the Knight always compelled him to look. Was it because he was lonely and wanted…His thoughts faded away.

Tom opened his eyes and blinked and the fire came into focus, it needed another log putting on. Sitting contentedly watching the fire, feeling the warmth he thought how life had been good to him. He'd managed to get through his allotted years pretty well, enjoyed his work on the land and over the last few years loved going out for his walk to the hill each day. He suddenly felt Rosie nudging his arm and looking down at her, he smoothed her soft, silky head. "It's all right girl, I'm fine." Adding, "Everything's good."

*

X

The spidery bare branches of the weeping willow dangled lifelessly over the partly frozen water of the duck pond. Beneath the wispy branches, a few ducks struggled to paddle through the icy water and calling his dogs to heel the Baronet continued towards the narrow passageway leading to the church grounds.

Winter had arrived early and standing on the hill top Sir Edward stared out over the winter landscape. It was bitterly cold and it reminded him of his first year on the estate, no one could forget the big freeze of the early sixties. When he was on his way down from Scotland, he remembered seeing small villages cut off by large snowdrifts. The snow ploughs too busy working on the main roads to tackle smaller ones.

He had inherited the estate along with the title from his older brother and he wondered what he had taken on. Their ancestors had owned the land for centuries and now it was in his hands and the responsibility sometimes weighed heavily upon him.

Over the years, Edward had given much thought on how to bring the estate into the modern world without being too brutal, destroying the beauty and charm of the area or upsetting his tenants. He knew them all well some like his longest working tenant farmer had lived in the village all his life, long before he'd inherited the estate and he suddenly wondered would younger tenants still be attracted to live and rent properties on the estate, especially when in this day and age to own your own home was the big dream.

He wanted his son young Edward known as Ned to carry on where he left off with at least some hope for the future. What income could be generated, to help with the repairs and upkeep needed, this was the problem and sometimes it seemed an endless task. He supposed it was the same for all landowners, especially now. The world was changing so fast, England had just elected their first woman as Prime Minister and he was not sure how he really felt about it although he tried hard to be fair. He had to admit Margaret Thatcher was certainly a strong individual.

He drew the collar of his waxed jacket up around his ears to keep out the wind, glad to have his old tweed cap on. His Labradors sat close to him, waiting patiently for him to move as he scanned the horizon and his eyes fell onto the avenue of trees either side of the narrow road that lead down into the village. Harry had the old trees replaced as repeated storms and severe winds had taken their toll on the older ones. He thought the young trees looked strong and healthy, a welcome sight when driving down between them off the main road, especially in spring with their new fresh green growth.

Looking across from his vantage point, he saw the outbuildings no longer used across the lane and he wondered how to put them to good use. It struck him they could be turned into a small shop selling home produce for the many visitors who came to see the village and he decided to give it some serious thought. He began to feel he was definitely making good progress.

Sir Edward loved to stand on the hill looking down on the land knowing it had been in his family for generations. That morning for some reason, he decided to go inside the church and he bid his dogs to sit and stay in the porch as he opened the heavy wooden door. The church was used every Sunday morning although these days they had to share the vicar with the other villages in the parish. The musty smell hit him straight away as he stepped inside the ancient building. Shutting the door behind him, it took a few minutes for his eyes to adjust to the gloom and he searched for the switches near the door to put the lights on.

Walking up the centre aisle towards the chancel arch, Edward was immediately drawn towards the large family memorial on the left hand side. He often wondered if his ancestors really looked anything like the carved figures kneeling there. He then remembered the story told of a secret passage. Some thought it began below the memorial or so the rumours went, but he was not convinced and like many, he thought if there was a secret passage someone would have found the exit by now let alone where it started from.

He wandered towards the chancel arch and stood looking at the altar with the lovely stained glass window above, his eyes fell onto the altar rails made of good solid oak. He looked at the memorial tablets and brass plaques around the chancel wall all to members of his family. He stood a few moments in front of the altar and then bowed his head before walking slowly back towards the door.

Outside in the porch the dogs jumped up wagging their tails pleased to see him as soon as he stepped through the doorway. As he left the porch, he felt the biting wind and once again pulled his collar up as high as it would go, the dogs stood close to his side until he gave the command and they set off smartly looking behind to see if he was following.

He passed the narrow window in the tower with the carved head above and did what everyone was inclined to do; he stopped and stared at it. He was suddenly struck by a thought before moving on, was the entrance to the passage in the four-foot thick walls. He studied the blocks of stone beneath the loophole window looking to see if there was any clue. There was nothing he could see or feel and he stood beneath the window looking thoughtfully towards the yew trees muttering under his breath before setting off down the path. "Nothing at all to be seen." He set off and the dogs happily ran ahead knowing where they were going and rubbing his cold hands together Sir Edward's thoughts were suddenly on the warmth of the large open fire at home.

*

December came in crisp and cold with clear, cloudless morning where the black, lacy outlines of distant trees stood out against the sky. Tom stayed in the warm, Maggie and Liz moved the bird table right in front of Tom's window, as near as they could, so he could watch what the birds were doing easily from his chair, it was one of his daily pleasures.

The jackdaws were the smartest and most interesting birds to watch as they perched nearby waiting for the main chance. They knew exactly how to scatter the smaller birds, swooping down to snatch any titbit they fancied before flying off with strong wings showing the familiar glossy black plumage. Many farmers hated them, calling them pests like the crows, or pigeons, something to be got rid of but Tom couldn't help feeling a certain admiration for clever birds and he watched them as they squabbled together like naughty children.

Each day became a bonus for Tom and over the weeks before Christmas although it was becoming difficult for him to stay awake for long he tried hard to tell each of his offspring how proud he was of them. He knew he was running out of time and it made him happy to see them all getting on with their lives. He just missed going for his daily walk every day with Rosie up on his hill to look out over the scene below as he always had done.

When Jen returned home to the village, she soon came to see him and he was more than pleased. He was so eager to ask her about Glyn.

"Have you seen Glyn yet?"

She smiled and nodded. "Yes and Nell; in fact she told me to tell you she'll be coming to see you soon." She laughed. "Everything's good, Granddad. You just rest and don't worry, Glyn and I are fine."

"Bring him to see me, Jen." He spoke slowly trying to get the words out straight. "I know he's busy with the farm but I would like to see him."

She bent down and kissed his old weathered cheek.

The following evening, Joe called to see Tom just as Liz came into the room and she gave Joe a big smile asking if he had thought about their offer. Tom looked at him eagerly as Liz went on. "We could do with a lodger, Joe you'd be doing us a favour." After a pause, she added, not wanting to sound too pushy.

Joe looked at them both. "It's a tempting offer."

"Maggie thinks it could work and if not, you can always opt for a different solution; maybe rent another cottage. The estate will find you somewhere in the village if you would rather. Anyway, we can give it a try for a while until you find out what you really want to do. We don't want you to leave, Joe."

Joe nodded. "Aye I know, I don't want to leave the village either. It's something to think about."

"Even Owen thinks it a good idea," added Liz. "So give us your final answer when you've made your mind up."

Joe sat with Tom for a while telling him about his ideas for the garden in spring until he saw the old man's eyes beginning to shut and he quietly went out and closed the door behind him.

A few days later, Jen brought Glyn around to see Tom and it gladdened his old heart to see the two of them together. He held his shaky hand out.

"How are you, Glyn lad? How's the farm these days?"

"Doing all right, Tom. I've got it all sorted, although you know we farmers could always do with better weather. Nell said to tell you she's coming to see you tomorrow." Glyn gave a chuckle and his eyes twinkled and Tom could see his Grandmother in him. "There's no stopping her, Tom."

Tom felt as if he had no energy and looking out of the window at the dreary sky after the doctor had called to see him, Tom heard a knock on the door.

"Are you awake? Can I come in, Tom?"

"Aye; glad you're here, Nell. I need a bit of cheering," he replied brightening up. "Tell me something cheery from the old days." His speech was definitely slower and it hurt her to hear him this way. "Let me think then." She shut her eyes thinking hard and after a few minutes said, "Do you remember that winter, Tom? The one when we were about thirteen, I thought I was so grown up and we were in the church porch? Do you remember the day it snowed?"

He nodded thinking hard, it was a freezing afternoon with a sharp wind and it started to sleet heavily and the sleet quickly turned to snow. Nell and Tom had squeezed into the corner of the porch, sitting on the ledge out of the wind to try and keep warm as they waited for it to ease off a bit. Being so close together Tom turned his head towards her and tried in vain to kiss her. Although he was only a year younger, Nell thought of him as a mere boy and at the time, she was already sweet on William who was older and more dashing. She knew Tom meant nothing by his advances and was only practising so she elbowed him and pushed him with one word: "Off!"

Poor Tom had been more than stunned by her reaction and he nearly fell off the ledge. Her elbow was bony and hard but he shrugged his shoulders and shuffled his feet until suddenly Nell saw the funny side and the pair of them ended up laughing until tears rolled down her cheeks and Tom was doubled up with the stitch.

"You were always cruel 'our Nell'." And the memory of that episode cheered him up completely.

Nell sat looking at Tom as his eyes closed and his head sank on his chest as he dropped off to sleep. She thought to herself, *I'll leave him enjoy a five minute nap before I wake him*. She sat there and suddenly noticed the photograph of William on the mantle-shelf above and wondered if she should tell Tom what really happened between them. No, she decided against it, it wouldn't do Tom any good.

It brought it all back to her. She had been so jealous when Tom asked Meg to marry him. She remembered thinking, Tom was her best friend not Meg's; how could he. She didn't want to marry him herself, but didn't want Meg or anyone else to marry him either. What a spoilt girl I must have been, she thought, and she suddenly laughed and I was going to marry poor William come what may. She could see his face so clearly when she asked him, so startled with a look of complete panic. He made her so cross the way he said 'No' she flew at him, temper out of control and she winced, thinking of the hard smack on his face she gave him, a fatal mistake. Gritting his teeth, he turned on his heel and she remembered him walking smartly down the path leaving her up on the hilltop. She remembered being bitterly upset and angry, not only with William but with her-self and from that day until he came home wounded from the war, they ignored each other.

When he returned home in a pitiful state, although she was married to Jack, she rushed to see him straight desperately sorry and to try and help. She always thought of him with sadness remembering the time he told her how relieved he'd felt when he heard she'd married Jack as he often worried about her. He then said he wished he had found someone to love, but now he was glad he hadn't because he knew it was too late and he looked so sad when he said it; it broke her heart.

She thought how later she had rushed down the lane and headed up to the hilltop. She stood there for some time thinking of some of the things he said and realised there was more to it than she knew. When she felt calmer, she thought how poor William never really had much of a chance, like thousands who went off to war; they had no chance at all.

Tom looked at Nell and wondered why she looked sad, but as soon as she saw he was awake, she brightened up and gave a wicked laugh.

"I've been thinking, those were the days, Tom, when I thought maybe I could marry you." She squeezed his hand. "You know I love you and always will but not in that way. I was just totally jealous of you picking Meg not me. It was only later I realised you were not only meant for each other but had good reason to be wed anyway." She laughed again.

"Remember I went to work on the farm and met my Jack. It changed everything for me. Remember how laid back he was with that dry sense of humour but he was such a passionate man who took no nonsense from me and yes I did tell him all about William and you. He just laughed out loud and shook his head saying I would have given you hell. He was right, I would have."

Nell went on, "But you know when William came home how I felt bad about us falling out" – she paused – "I went to see him straight away to see if I could be of help and I desperately wanted to say how sorry I was and make amends. It really hurt me to see him; we had once been so close. We were all close back in those days. Oh Tom!" Her face sagged and she suddenly looked her age. "Where has the time gone?"

The weather took a turn for the worse with heavy snow forecast. Tom sat in his chair by the fire and thought of the days he worked out in the fields in bitter December weather, trudging through snow, breaking the ice on the water troughs for the cattle and sheep. He remembered standing on the hill with the sound of the wind whipping fiercely around the tower causing the yews to wail and creak.

As a farmer, he knew there was nothing like a harsh winter with heavy frosts to break up the clods of earth left after the autumn ploughing. A freezing winter made for perfect soil in spring and he couldn't help feeling a few nostalgic thoughts for those days although the reality was different. Painful chilblains and chapped hands so bad Meg had to help him, putting Vaseline on at night to try and ease the severe splits in his fingers. He looked up at the window and saw it had started to snow.

A silence fell over the land as the snowflakes large and luminous slowly fell increasing within minutes to a heavy fall, the snow so dense Tom could not see out through his window. With the cold weather, his health did not improve but as Christmas was upon them, he made an effort for the festive season.

Six of them sat around the table in the kitchen for Christmas dinner. Tom at one end in his wheelchair, he said it was easier. Owen sat opposite him, Maggie and Kath sat one side and Liz and Joe the other. It was a jolly meal complete with festive hats and crackers and the traditional bringing to the table of the Christmas pudding with its sprig of holly on top, set alight with brandy. Owen wheeled Tom off after dinner was over to his easy chair so he could put his feet up and have a quiet snooze. He felt unusually quiet and sat in his room watching the birds through the window almost like someone watching a slow motion film on the television. He wondered why he felt so strange.

Christmas afternoon passed quickly. Laura arrived plump and glowing as she came into the kitchen through the scullery door followed by the rest of the family. The two boys went in to see if their Grandad Tom was awake after his rest and Alex happily stayed with him for a while in front of the fire along with Rosie. Jen and Glyn arrived to wish him a 'Merry Christmas'.

When Joe came in later to fetch him for Christmas Tea, he told Tom he'd decided to stay where he was in the little cottage and renew his lease. Tom's face fell until Joe continued by telling him. "I'll still be here, Tom, to help with the garden. I'll not be going anywhere." Tom nodded and looked a bit more cheerful as Joe wheeled him in to join the others.

After tea, Tom called it a day and withdrew to his room leaving them all to an evening of games and listening to the fire crackling his eyes searched out Meg's photograph. "It's been a good Christmas day, Meg. Aye, it's been grand to be with the family."

Christmas had always been a happy, homely time and Tom had warm vague memories of past times and he sat there thinking. There was always a lot of activity going on, the making of paper chains and lanterns for weeks to hang on the Christmas tree bought from the market square and the hanging up of the well darned wool stockings on Christmas Eve before bed.

There was not much money in those days but Christmas morning, the stockings were filled with lumpy packages, mostly home-made by Meg, wrapped and tied with red or green string. He remembered Meg made sure they always had something new to wear and there were packets of toffee and usually in the toe of each sock a few nuts and a small apple or orange if they were lucky.

Suddenly, Tom thought of one special Christmas when they were very young he called Owen and the girls to look outside. He pointed to the small tree opposite the back door and there on the bare branches hung apples, pears, walnuts and oranges, amongst brightly coloured stars. They hung there like magic, spinning around. He remembered watching as they stood awestruck with their mouths open and they could choose any fruit they wanted from the magic tree.

Meg had worked secretly at night to make the neatly sewn stars out of scraps of bright red and green material and scrimped and saved to buy extra fruit and walnuts. He had climbed his stepladder that Christmas Eve in the bitter cold to hang everything on the tree and although Tom often had a hard time with his memory he suddenly saw that tree in glorious detail. He suddenly hankered for the past wishing he could go back for a while.

Closing his eyes, he remembered the first time he met Meg. Nell introduced her to him after church and the three of them walked together to the brow of the hill. He remembered thinking of her as a rather plain girl to begin with, but before she left to go home, she looked up at him with her large serious eyes and gave him one of her stunning smiles as she said goodbye and he was so taken aback he forgot to reply and was left staring after her as she and Nell went down the path towards the gate.

Lulled by the warm fire and warm thoughts of Meg, Tom fell asleep and saw himself with his old sheepdog Connie, once his faithful companion long before Rosie and Jess. As they stood up on the hill snow began to fall, it obscured everything and the wind started to blow the snowflakes in flurries and he held tightly onto his old tweed cap to stop it blowing away and Connie followed behind him as he hurried around the tower looking for cover.

He passed the carved head above the window as he hurried into the porch when he suddenly saw a figure walking towards him. It was William looking tall and handsome just as he looked before the war and Tom's heart leapt as he moved joyfully towards him, hand outstretched but the snow was so heavy he lost sight of him and was left calling his name.

Tom opened his eyes and sighed as he stared into the fire. The snow in his dream reminded him of the December they had a deep fall of snow and he and William went sledging late one afternoon. They decided to try the sledge from the church side gate, down between the dry stonewalls, where the snow had been compacted to a sheet of ice. William said as he was the oldest he would sit in the front to steer. They got on the sledge, counted three and shot down the slope. Tom remembered being scared as he and William shot straight through the opening and disappeared over the grassy bank, across the lane and landed with William's feet in the village pond, water up to his knees and no sign of the sledge. Luckily, Tom had fallen off with no damage.

The old boy who lived in the cottage where Ted and Mary lived, rushed out waving his stick calling them all the young fools he could lay his tongue to. They ran off home as quick as they could leaving the sledge in the pond and had to face their angry mother over William's saturated boots and their father for being so stupid and reckless beside leaving the wooden sledge in the pond. He was furious saying one of them could have drowned.

Tom suddenly heard a voice calling him and opening his eyes he saw young Alex by the door with the others standing behind him.

"We've come to see you to say good night and 'Merry Christmas', Grandad Tom. We have to go now but I'll see you soon."

He went to the old man and Tom took his hand and shook it warmly.

"Aye, that you will, lad." And he added, "Merry Christmas all of you."

*

XI

It was a bright winter morning and a sharp breeze blew down the green valley around the old chimney pots and continued along the lane to the hill. A jet flew across the sky with a high-pitched scream and hurtled out of sight leaving a long white trail behind. The rooks rising up into the air squawked loudly frightened by the noise and as they settled, back down a silence fell over the wood behind the hall.

Perched on top of the tower, a large bird sat and watched, the sharp eyes searched for any movement down in the grass; something darted out in panic. Opening its wings, the bird noiselessly lifted into the air and swooped catching its prey before flying off into the distance.

Young Ned stood beneath the carved head of the Knight staring at the yew trees but his thoughts were elsewhere. He was disturbed by the fact some of his acquaintances were already in negotiations with various groups to sell all or part of their estates. His own lands were definitely not for sale although his running costs were hard to handle. He would definitely not be making any deal. The land had been in his family ever since the twelfth century, he just could not do it.

He had managed to improve the running of his estate and now there was some hope of a new lucrative sideline. He had just interested a television company in filming at the Manor with talk of a major documentary already in the pipeline. The Manor would be advertised through a website like other stately homes and he was already thinking of using it as a venue for various large functions. Along with the guided tours in summer, he hoped this would bring in a good return and he began to feel more than hopeful.

There were a few small businesses set up in the village and they were doing well and the remaining working farms were reasonably profitable for the time being. He suddenly thought of old Tom still living at Oldfield farm, the fields once used by him now rented out to younger farmers. Many farmers had turned to growing a certain amount of 'oilseed rape' as it was more profitable.

Ned knew Tom, Maggie and Liz were content looking after their farm as they had always done and he was pleased Joe was helping them with the garden. Tom was getting frailer and who knew what the near future held. He had called to see Tom the day before and told him how he missed him sitting on his wooden seat at the side of the church porch and it had pleased Tom to know he was missed by young Sir Edward.

The changes the old boy must have seen over his ninety odd years of living in the village and Ned wondered how much time Tom really had left. He often asked him what the secret of his long life was and Tom just laughed and shook his head telling him 'Perhaps working hard and being content'.

Ned watched his two boys as they suddenly appeared and ran up the path towards him and he wondered what the future held for them. He hoped that one or both of them would take over from him when the time came and they would take their responsibilities just as seriously as their forebears, but he knew life was not as simple as that, the future was never really predictable.

The New Year was upon them already and he couldn't believe where time had gone. The world was changing so quickly and he thought, with all the new technology it could possibly be the most exciting time ever. Then he smiled to himself thinking it was difficult to keep up with everything, his boys would probably find it much easier. He looked down at them affectionately and for once, they were standing still by his side, in front of the tower, the dogs either side of them quietly waiting.

"Look, I can see a pheasant, Dad."

The younger child became excited. "Look, Dad. Shall we catch it?" He pointed at the beautifully coloured bird with its red wattle and magnificent tail moving slowly through the grass alongside the running water. The bird blissfully unaware it was being observed continued to strut along looking for this or that. The Baronet looked where the boy pointed and for a moment, a tinge of sadness crept over him as he wondered if there would always be pheasants strolling through the village and he suddenly wanted everything to stay exactly the same, although he well knew nothing ever did and suddenly felt a deep sadness.

"Come on, Dad. We'll race you home." The boy tugged at Ned's sleeve as he jumped around him full of energy and they ran down the hill the dogs barking loudly behind them. The pheasant disappeared out of sight and the hill was left in silence. The clouds drifted across the sky, slowly passing over the yew trees and the carved head above the small window looked towards the yews.

*

Tom was ordered to stay in bed and the week went by slowly and about four in the afternoon on New Year's Eve, Tess brought Nell down to see him and she sat waiting for him to wake up. As she sat staring out of the window, it started to snow again and she looked at the big flakes as they fell slowly down and she knew this time it was going to be a heavy fall. It was already starting to get dark and the world was silent with the dark heavy clouds low in the sky. Everything had scurried out of sight and Tom suddenly opened his eyes and looked at her.

"Tess brought me for five minutes," she said. "It's really snowing, Tom, I just wanted to be the first to wish you a Happy New Year even if it is a few hours early."

She patted his arm and held his hand. He looked at her without saying anything. He managed a smile.

Tess put her head around the door. "It's time, Mum; we must go before the weather gets any worse."

"Happy New Year, Tom," Nell whispered. "See you soon."

Tom's eyes opened wide and he beckoned her closer. "Nell." His voice was no more than a whisper; with an effort, he continued, "I'll wait for you; then we'll all be up on the hill together." He mouthed the words but there was little sound.

She looked at him and replied, "Aye, Tom, wait and I'll be there." With that, Nell left the room, Tess shutting the door quietly behind her and without looking at her daughter, Nell wept.

At five minutes to midnight, Maggie put her head around the door to see if Tom was awake. She checked the fire and Liz joined her just as the clock struck twelve, Tom stirred. They gently told him the New Year had arrived and his eyes opened with almost a gleam of enthusiasm; he replied quite clearly, "Has it." And he shut his eyes once more drifting in and out.

He felt relieved he had made it to the New Year, he couldn't remember which year it was but somehow it had arrived.

Meg looked up at him. "Happy New Year, Tom." He could see her sitting curled up on the sofa next to him. Big Ben had struck midnight. Meg had not been well that week so they stayed home and didn't go to the village hall. Tom remembered how calm he felt, they had accepted what was inevitable and they sat by the fire together as the New Year arrived and lifting his head up off the pillow his eyes looked around for her.

In the following week, Owen and Kath sat with him as often as they could to give Maggie and Liz a break. Joe came in each day to see him always reporting on the progress of the garden. He wasn't sure Tom understood what he was telling him but felt he wanted to let him know his garden was doing well. Jenny came with Glyn to say their goodbye.

Mark and Alex came to see him with Laura and Ben. Alex sat close to his Granddad Tom and watched him intently weighing up what was happening. Tom opened his eyes briefly and looked at Alex; he managed to give him a reassuring smile to say all was well and the boy seemed to understand and unafraid he held his great grandfather's hand and tried to smile back. Rosie refused to leave the room, she usually lay at the side of the bed but that morning she sat and rested her head on the bed itself as near as she could to Tom's hand. He tried to stroke the soft fur.

He asked Maggie to fetch Nell and came straight away to sit by him, someone once told him at the very end you saw your whole life flash before you and looking up at Nell and the family he closed his eyes. He found himself walking jauntily down the lane without his stick, continuing up the path passing the village hall, heading towards the side gate of the church grounds, he was on his way. Going through the gate, he saw the majestic yews swaying gently and he noticed a few early snowdrops here and there. Walking past his seat, he looked up at the Knight above the window who seemed to be looking at him as if was waiting for him. Tom suddenly felt young and strong as he happily stood on the hilltop. He was ready, ready to be with Meg and the others, they would all wait for Nell together and breathing in deeply he took a step into his future before letting his breath slowly and silently escape.

*

XII

The moon was still visible; a pale shadow of its former self in the early morning sky. The wind was sharp blowing from the northeast. Calling his dogs to heel, Ned set off briskly down the lane heading towards the path leading up to the church. He stood in front of the tower and breathed in the cold morning air admiring the lovely setting of his manor residence; it never failed to please him.

Going around the side of the church, he reverently walked around the old graves past the base of the Saxon cross and made his way to where Tom was laid to rest some weeks ago. He stood looking at the dates 1908–2001 and noticed the fresh flowers recently laid there along with the fading wreaths. As the sun broke through the clouds, it made the morning sky pink with streaks of red. Although it was said to be a sign of bad weather ahead, it bathed the church grounds in a soft warm colour and the Baronet murmured to himself, "Not a bad place to be, Tom. Not bad."

On his way back to the front of the tower, he stopped to look across the adjoining field and noticed where the stonewall was crumbling and made a mental note to get someone to repair it before it got worse and he decided to go and stand a while in his favourite place on the brow of the hill before starting his daily work.

February was bitterly cold and it was sharp standing on the hilltop, he suddenly felt the bitingly cold wind whip around him and he stepped back between the strong buttresses for shelter. He stood a few moments listening to the noisy rooks flying above the wood behind the hall a familiar sight seen many times. As the birds settled down and disappeared out of sight, silence surrounded him and wrapped in quietness, he felt the sad lonely feeling he sometimes felt as he realised the past always slips away.

Staring at the peaceful scene in front of him, he remembered his new tenants were moving into the village the following week and thought the old had passed on, now the new were moving in and cheered he stepped out into the cold morning ready to get on with his day.

Sitting on Tom's seat, Nell waited for Tess who was with Maggie and Liz. Nell had wanted some time on her own and Tess said she wouldn't be long.

"Oh, Tom," Nell muttered under her breath. "First William, then Meg, then my Jack and now you, it seems only yesterday we were so young and full of life always meeting up here laughing and playful." She had taken it hard when William and Meg went and then her Jack, now, her oldest and dearest friend, Tom, had gone and although she missed them all, somehow she missed Tom more than she cared to say. Pulling herself together, she got up with difficulty using her walking sticks. She felt cold and decided to walk slowly to meet Tess. Looking up at the carved head of the Knight above, she thought, *At least you're still here,* and then said out loud, "I hope your all waiting for me, Tom, like you said." And looking at the seat added, "We can all meet right her."

Standing in front of the tower, Ned heard the sound of a few birds bravely pretending it was spring and he felt a surge of optimism. What did the year 2001 offer? Although it was still hovering around freezing, there were signs of new growth appearing everywhere. He stood for a while enjoying the view below in the early morning and he whistled the dogs to heel, they immediately ran to him and sat down by his side. He loved these early mornings and breathing in the fresh cold air, it felt good to be alive.

Closely followed by the dogs, he quickly walked around the church heading for the worn signpost pointing to the footpath that lead across the fields. Moving reverently around the graves, he stopped to read a few of the names and dates. Many of his forebears were buried around the grounds some had large ornate graves whilst others simple gravestones, covered in lichen and moss, hard to read. He remembered many of his ancestors were interred down in the crypt beneath the church, out of sight and out of mind. His own choice was definitely to be on the hill beneath the sky. And suddenly thinking warmly of old Tom as he passed by where he was recently buried, he stopped to linger a few moments before setting off across the fields for his walk.

The weather turned milder and wetter that afternoon and water dripped from the top of the tower, cascading over the dark grey blocks of stone. Ned walked down the lane opposite the pond and turned up to the side gate of the church. He immediately felt the quiet atmosphere as he stepped into the church grounds. It was late afternoon and he was pleased to have finished the task he was doing, enjoying a little time to himself before he headed home. He noticed the wet gravestones as he passed by, some looking as if they were nestling in the long grass. The grass itself was saturated and the branches of the yew trees hung heavy, water dripping onto him as he passed underneath them.

He headed towards the old seat beneath the loophole window and bent down to read the recently added shiny new brass plaque that simply said in capital letters 'TOM' and he sat down for a few moments to remember his oldest tenant and couldn't believe how quickly the weeks had flown by. Watching the branches of the yew trees begin to sway gently to and fro, he said, "Look at that, Tom." Strangely, he felt as if old Tom was sitting there alongside him.

Shaking his head, he got up to go on his way and turned automatically to look at the worn features of the carved head above the widow, as always it looked calmly towards the yews, all was in its rightful place. He would go and stand in front of the tower as the wind picked up and he pulled the collar of his coat up higher for warmth. Looking over his land, head high, he stood a tall, upright figure looking out into the distance as the sun slipped down out of sight and the evening shadows crept slowly over the hill.

The End